LETHAL WEDDING

CHARLOTTE BYRD

CHARLOTTE BYRD
dangerously addictive

Identifiers

ISBN (e-book): 978-1-63225-111-4

ISBN (paperback): 978-1-63225-112-1

❀ Created with Vellum

ABOUT LETHAL WEDDING
(WEDLOCKED TRILOGY BOOK 2)

To save my father's life and our family's legacy, I have to marry a cruel man who wants me only as a trophy.

I thought Franklin Parks was a bad man before, but now I know he's a monster.

To survive, I will have to beat him at his own game. But then Henry Asher, my one and only love, comes back into my life and things get a lot more complicated.

Franklin is not only my fiancé but also

Henry's boss, and he will stop at nothing to get **everything** he wants…

Henry Asher

I was a fool to let her go. Now, I'll have to do everything to get her back…

Aurora never thought I could be a rich dirtbag who would do anything to get what he wants but I am proving her wrong.

To help her, I had to teach myself a few things.

To protect her, I had to become my worst enemy.

To save her, I will have to do the unthinkable.

The problem is that she doesn't want saving. She has her own plans. But the wedding is approaching and time is running out…

Read the SECOND book to the

addictive *WEDLOCKED* series by bestselling author *Charlotte Byrd.*

What readers are saying about Charlotte Byrd:

"This book/series is addictive! Super hot and steamy, intense with twists and turns in the plot that you just won't see coming…" Amazon review ★★★★★

"This series is just so **intense and delicious.** The stunning twists, raw emotions and nerve wracking tension just keep increasing as each book in this enticing series unfolds. I am so invested in Nicholas and Olivia. These characters really worm their way into your heart, while also totally consuming your mind. The gripping story quickly captivates and pulls you back into this couple's world." Amazon review ★★★★★

"Extremely captivating, sexy, steamy, intriguing, and intense!" ★★★★★

"Addictive and impossible to put down."
★★★★★

"I can't get enough of the turmoil, lust, love, drama and secrets!" ★★★★★

"Fast-paced romantic suspense filled twists and turns, danger, betrayal and so much more." ★★★★★

"Decadent, delicious, & dangerously addictive!" ★★★★★

PRAISE FOR CHARLOTTE BYRD

"BEST AUTHOR YET! Charlotte has done it again! There is a reason she is an amazing author and she continues to prove it! I was definitely not disappointed in this series!!" ★★★★★

"LOVE!!! I loved this book and the whole series!!! I just wish it didn't have to end. I am definitely a fan for life!!! ★★★★★

"Extremely captivating, sexy, steamy, intriguing, and intense!" ★★★★★

"Addictive and impossible to put down." ★★★★★

"What a magnificent story from the 1st book through book 6 it never slowed down always surprising the reader in one way or the other. Nicholas and Olive's paths crossed in a most unorthodox way and that's how their story begins it's exhilarating with that nail biting suspense that keeps you riding on the edge the whole series. You'll love it!"

★★★★★

"What is Love Worth. This is a great epic ending to this series. Nicholas and Olive have a deep connection and the mystery surrounding the deaths of the people he is accused of murdering is to be read. Olive is one strong woman with deep convictions. The twists, angst, confusion is all put together to make this worthwhile read."

★★★★★

"Fast-paced romantic suspense filled with twists and turns, danger, betrayal, and so much more." ★★★★★

"Decadent, delicious, & dangerously addictive!" - Amazon Review ★★★★★

"Titillation so masterfully woven, no reader can resist its pull. A MUST-BUY!" - Bobbi Koe, Amazon Review

★★★★★

"Captivating!" - Crystal Jones, Amazon Review ★★★★★

"Sexy, secretive, pulsating chemistry…" - Mrs. K, Amazon Reviewer ★★★★★

"Charlotte Byrd is a brilliant writer. I've read loads and I've laughed and cried. She writes a balanced book with brilliant characters. Well done!" -Amazon Review ★★★★★

"Hot, steamy, and a great storyline." - Christine Reese ★★★★★

"My oh my....Charlotte has made me a fan for life." - JJ, Amazon Reviewer ★★★★★

"Wow. Just wow. Charlotte Byrd leaves me speechless and humble… It definitely kept me on the edge of my seat. Once you pick it up, you won't put it down." - Amazon Review ★★★★★

" Intrigue, lust, and great characters...what more could you ask for?!" - Dragonfly Lady ★★★★★

WANT TO BE THE FIRST TO KNOW ABOUT MY UPCOMING SALES, NEW RELEASES AND EXCLUSIVE GIVEAWAYS?

Sign up for my newsletter: https://www.subscribepage.com/byrdVIPList

Join my Facebook Group: https://www.facebook.com/groups/276340079439433/

Bonus Points: Follow me on BookBub and Goodreads!

ABOUT CHARLOTTE BYRD

Charlotte Byrd is the bestselling author of romantic suspense novels. She has sold over 600,000 books and has been translated into five languages.

She lives near Palm Springs, California with her husband, son, and a toy Australian Shepherd. Charlotte is addicted to books and Netflix and she loves hot weather and crystal blue water.

Write her here:

charlotte@charlotte-byrd.com

Check out her books here:

www.charlotte-byrd.com

Connect with her here:

www.facebook.com/charlottebyrdbooks

www.instagram.com/charlottebyrdbooks

www.twitter.com/byrdauthor

Want to hear about new releases, free books and get exclusive giveaways?

Sign up for my newsletter!

Sign up for my newsletter: https://www. subscribepage.com/byrdVIPList

Join my Facebook Group: https://www. facebook.com/groups/276340079439433/

Bonus Points: Follow me on BookBub and Goodreads!

facebook.com/charlottebyrdbooks

twitter.com/byrdauthor

instagram.com/charlottebyrdbooks

bookbub.com/profile/charlotte-byrd

ALSO BY CHARLOTTE BYRD

All books are available at ALL major retailers! If you can't find it, please email me at charlotte@charlotte-byrd.com

Wedlocked Trilogy
Dangerous Engagement
Lethal Wedding
Fatal Wedding

Tell me Series
Tell Me to Stop
Tell Me to Go
Tell Me to Stay

Tell Me to Run
Tell Me to Fight
Tell Me to Lie

Tangled Series

Tangled up in Ice
Tangled up in Pain
Tangled up in Lace
Tangled up in Hate
Tangled up in Love

Black Series

Black Edge
Black Rules
Black Bounds
Black Contract
Black Limit

Lavish Trilogy

Lavish Lies
Lavish Betrayal
Lavish Obsession

Standalone Novels

Debt

Offer

Unknown

Dressing Mr. Dalton

1

HENRY

I watch her from afar. I follow her down the street.

I see her laughing, tossing her hair back. She smiles and disappears around the corner.

I see her moments later with her face buried in her phone. She's reading my message but she's not replying.

I have called her a number of times, too many to count. I don't want to be a stalker and yet here I am, watching her, following her, forcing myself into her world.

I know that what I am doing is wrong, but I can't stop it.

I want her back.

I need her back.

My life doesn't make sense without her.

Does hers make sense without me?

When Aurora stops outside a store, she stands with her arms crossed peering at the books behind the glass. Tempted to approach her, I imagine myself walking up to her and giving her a hug and a kiss as if she were still mine.

I press my fingertips into my palms and notice the whites of my knuckles. I take a deep breath even though my chest tightens along with my windpipe.

The next breath is just as laborious, if not more so. It takes everything in me to pull myself away from her.

Aurora doesn't know that I am in New York because I shouldn't be here.

No one knows that I'm here. Not my editor, not my boss, not my boss's boss. I flew here from Kentucky on my own dime and I have to be back at LaGuardia airport tonight.

That's all the time that I have to figure out what to do, or perhaps what not to do. When I got the ticket, I thought that I would come here and find her and tell her that I love her and we should get back together. But watching her ignore my calls and my texts, I don't think I have the strength to face a rejection face-to-face.

Aurora and I had a fight, one of many, which resulted from distance and pain and loneliness. We let our frustrations push us apart, and I regret ever saying that I wanted to take a break.

At first, she was upset. She called me a few times and I let those calls go to voice mail.

When it was my turn to call, it was her turn to push me away.

I'd like to say that I don't believe in regrets because it's a cool thing to say.

It's as if in today's world, we should all embrace every stupid thing that we have ever done just because these moments are the ones that have 'made you the person that you are today'.

But the truth is that I don't believe in any of that.

It's bullshit.

Not everything that I have ever done

contributed to me becoming a better person. Many things were just fucked up and unnecessary and plain old mistakes that I wish I could take back.

Forgetting about Aurora's graduation, focusing too much on my work, and then telling her that I'm tired of us even though at that moment, I was just tired, are the mistakes that I wish I could take back.

Saying those words to her set everything in motion and now there is no going back.

I watch Aurora disappear into the bookstore and wish more than anything that I could follow her.

Yesterday, I thought that I would.

I thought that I would get off that plane and go straight to her house and tell her everything that I have been feeling ever since we broke up.

But now, I can't bring myself to do it.

It's not because I don't miss her. I miss her more than I have ever missed anyone.

Without her in my life, I feel like a part of me is gone.

If I were to suddenly lose a limb, I would probably miss it a lot less.

I touch the door to the bookstore, running my fingers over its ornate design. I grab the handle and hold it open for a customer with her hair slicked back into a severe bun.

I linger for a moment and then watch a customer walk out. She doesn't look up from her phone but gives me a brief nod, a thank you.

Go inside, I say to myself, go inside or you'll regret this the same way you regret everything else.

I take a deep breath and step over the threshold. I look for Aurora in the front near the registers and search for her through the aisles in the back.

The further back I go the more disorganized everything gets. The aisles are all labeled but most of the books are miscategorized and some are shelved with their spines in. I walk past aisle after aisle searching for her, finally spotting her all the way in the back, in the romance section.

Her shoulders move up and down with each breath as she turns the pages delicately.

Holding the book up to her face, Aurora's nose is quite literally buried in it.

"What are you doing?" she asks when I take a step and the floor makes a loud creaking sound.

"I wanted to talk to you," I say.

"So you followed me?"

"No, no, I mean yes," I stumble.

"Which is it?" Aurora cocks her head and narrows her eyes.

"Can we talk?" I ask.

"We are talking," she says.

She knows perfectly well that that's not what I mean, I don't know how to help her get past this angry part so that she will hear me out.

"You were supposed to be there," she says, walking around me and toward the register.

"I know, I'm really sorry." I rush after her. "I was just working on a story and I got really caught up with it."

"I know that you have this career that you are really passionate about, but I have my own life and my own drama and I thought that I could rely on my boyfriend to be there for me."

"You can," I say.

"Really?"

"I'm sorry," I say, taking a deep breath. "I know that I fucked up. I should have never suggested that we break up. But I tried to call you so many times afterward..."

I stand here next to her and wait for the cashier to run her credit card and for her to enter her pin number.

"I'm really sorry about how everything turned out," Aurora says when we get outside.

The rush of the traffic startles me for a moment. I have been in Kentucky for too long, I decide.

"So is this it?" I ask.

She shrugs.

"Do you not wanna talk about this anymore?"

She shrugs again.

Aurora puts the weight of her body on the back of her foot as if she's about to spin and walk away, but something stops her.

"What do you want to happen?" she asks.

"I want you back," I say without missing a beat. "I am really sorry about everything, especially about missing your graduation. I love you, Aurora. I miss you more than you could ever imagine. I need you back in my life."

Big fat tears start to well up in her eyes. Her face contorts as she tries to push them away.

Aurora covers her mouth with her hand and shakes her head mumbling, "No, no, no."

I reach over and put my arm around her, but she pushes me away.

"No, I can't," she says.

"Why not?" I whisper.

It feels like there's something that she is not telling me.

But the harder I push, the further away she gets.

"I have to go," she says, wiping her cheeks. "I can't see you again, Henry. Too much has happened."

2

HENRY

When she walks away, she takes my ability to breathe.

Is this what it feels like to die?

Folding in half, I wrap my hands around my knees and start to sob, not caring who can hear me.

I don't know how long I stay there. Eventually, I force myself up to my feet. I know that I'm pathetic, but with my heart shattering into a million little pieces, how should I act?

Should I just pretend that I'm fine?

Should I punch someone in the face?

Is that what a better man would do?

No, the only way out is to go through the pain, not around it, not over it, just directly through it. I know that, but that doesn't make it any easier.

I want to follow Aurora again.

I want to force her to tell me what happened.

I want to force her to take me back.

But sometimes, you reach this point and you just know that you can't push the other person any further.

I know her enough to know that what she said back there is her truth. The only way that I can find out what is really going on is by letting some time pass and to heal a little bit.

When I first got to New York and I saw her at her apartment and I followed her to that bookstore, I didn't want to approach her because I didn't want the last conversation that we had to be a breakup.

Unfortunately, I didn't listen to my own advice.

Now, we didn't just break up over the phone, she also dumped me in real life.

There goes another regret to add to that gigantic pile of regrets that is my life.

I pick up my phone and scroll through social media. When that's not enough of a distraction, I open the news app. Hours pass and I don't feel any better, but I do become too numb to process anything bad in any real way.

Then my phone rings. His name pops up on the screen: Jackie.

I'm tempted to let it go to voicemail, but I answer anyway. After a brief hello, I tell him that I'm actually in the city if he wants to get a drink.

Jackie Peterson is a friend of mine from Montauk. He was a year behind me in school and we weren't that close until after graduation.

It takes Jackie an hour to get to the bar I suggest and I'm already on my third glass of scotch.

"I don't drink anymore," he says, taking the seat next to me.

I raise my eyebrows at that revelation.

Jackie is the kind of guy who was always down for a good time.

"What are you talking about?" I ask.

He shrugs and orders a Coke with a wedge of lemon.

"Is it because you're working?" I ask.

"Well, I'm not supposed to drink on the job, but no it's not because of that. I quit drinking, and everything else, 375 days ago." He laughs.

"Wow, that's kind of a precise number."

"Yeah, I don't miss it one bit," he says, his voice drenched in sarcasm.

"Uh-huh." I nod.

"I'm just kidding," he adds. "In reality, you kind of count the days when it's the only thing you can think of when you wake up in the morning and when you go to bed at night and every other waking moment of the fucking day."

I look down at my glass and finish it quickly so as not to tempt him anymore. After handing the bartender my credit card, I invite Jackie for a cup of coffee.

"It's nice to see you again," Jackie says, taking a sip of his espresso at the shop on the corner. "What are you doing these days?"

"Working as a reporter," I say with a shrug. "I'm actually in town just for one day and I have to go back to Kentucky."

"Oh, really?" he asks. "I had no idea."

I expect him to ask me more about the type of stories that I'm working on, but when our eyes meet, I can see that he has something else on his mind.

Jackie is a tall guy with dark thick hair and broad shoulders and he can be quite charming and attractive, and the worst part is that he knows it.

He gives me a crooked smile and a wink.

"What is that?" I ask, sitting back in the big leather chair.

"Well, I've heard the rumors," he says slowly, savoring each word.

"What are you talking about?"

"About Aurora Penelope Tate," he says, enunciating each consonant in her name.

"I had no idea that you were so up on the gossip." I smile.

"Well, you know how it is, one of your old high school buddies starts dating an heir to a multi-billion dollar fortune and people start talking."

"There's nothing really to talk about," I say with a sigh. "We broke up."

"I'm sorry to hear that," he says, "but you knew that was going to happen, right?"

I shrug.

"Seriously?"

"Yes, this is the face of a man who knew that things weren't going to work out," I say.

"Okay, maybe not, but you didn't really expect to marry her, did you?"

His question takes me by surprise.

I stare at him, unsure as to how to react.

"Henry, come on man, tell me that you were just having a good time."

"I can't," I say, shaking my head. "That's the thing. Maybe I'm just an idiot but yes, I did think that we were going to end up together."

"No shit! Are you serious? I mean, were you two that serious?"

I give him a slight nod and look down into the blackness of my cup.

"That's why I'm in New York," I say. "I mean, we officially broke up earlier, but I flew all the way back here to try to make things right and she didn't want to hear it."

"Wow, I'm such an asshole," Jackie says, sitting back against his chair.

"Yes, you are."

"I really didn't mean to say any of —"

"Don't worry about it," I interrupt him.

"I'm-"

"Listen, let's just drop it. I don't really want to talk about it."

"I'm really sorry about this, man," Jackie says, putting his hand on my knee.

"Don't worry about it," I mumble.

I appreciate his support, but I'm a bit embarrassed at the same time.

Jackie and I aren't the types of friends to talk about anything serious that's going on in our lives. I feel dumb telling him all about any of this.

Also, I don't want him running back home and blabbing to everyone that we both know about how pathetic I am.

"That's really fucked up, man," Jackie says, finishing his coffee. "I wonder if that had anything to do with what happened to her dad."

I look up at him, my ears starting to buzz.

"What are you talking about?" I ask.

"Well, it was all over the news."

"What was?"

"I thought that you knew."

"No, I don't fucking know," I snap.

"Her dad got arrested," Jackie says. "They even had a perp walk for him."

I stare at him, dumbfounded.

"Perpetrator walk?" I ask.

"Yeah, you know, when the cops specifically call the media and walk the accused past the press so everyone can get those pictures and videos of him in handcuffs with his head hanging low."

"Yes, I know what a perp walk is," I say, urging him to continue. "What was he arrested for?"

"That I'm not so sure about," Jackie says. "Insider trading, I think. Isn't that the only thing that the rich elite ever get arrested for?"

I shake my head, uncertain as to what to think.

"There's more."

"What are you talking about?" I ask.

"Well, the thing is that right after the arrest, he had a heart attack. While in custody."

3

AURORA

I miss him more than I ever thought I would.

No, that's not entirely true. I knew that it would hurt. I just didn't realize it would hurt this much.

But we got so used to being apart.

It's not like we lived together and were with each other every single day. Still, my heart aches for Henry.

I think about him all the time, almost every minute of the day, and especially when I should be thinking about something else.

My father is in the hospital.

My father has been arrested.

My father has had a heart attack.

Yet all I can think about is Henry.

I want to see him and I want him to hold me and promise that everything is going to be alright.

When we first broke up, I waited for him to call me back. I wanted him to fix everything and to make everything better.

But he didn't.

He made me wait.

That made me angry.

When he finally called, texted, and called again, I didn't write back, not because I didn't want to but because I wanted him to suffer as much as I did.

And then something changed. After some time had passed, I couldn't bring myself to call him back even though I wanted to more than anything.

Each hour is just a blur of the one before.

I'm angry and mad and sad all at the same time.

I have no control over anything that's going on in my life.

I'm lost and anything that I try to do is not enough.

At the hospital, minutes and hours tick by at an excruciatingly slow pace. It doesn't help that my mother is omnipresent, like some sort of malevolent God who watches you all the time, waiting for you to screw up.

Nothing I have ever done has ever been good enough and that has never been clearer than it is now.

She's taking her anger out on me and there is only so much I can take. The one time that I escape for a casual walk down the street, and pop into a bookstore, to find something to take my mind off my shitty, shitty life, I run into him.

Henry has been following me.

He doesn't hide this fact.

He wants me to know.

A big part of me is happy, overjoyed even, to see him. I have missed him and just being in his presence is overwhelming.

Henry is as tall and gorgeous as ever, with his thick black curls and broad shoulders and that trustworthy Roman nose and piercing eyes.

He is one of the few guys in New York City who doesn't seem to know quite how attractive he is and the fact that he doesn't know makes him even more so.

He's humble in that way that people who are truly humble are, without pretense and without putting on airs.

When he corners me in one of the aisles, it takes everything within me not to run into his arms. I want to tell him that I forgive him and I want him to make everything better.

But I can't.

I can't do anything until I figure out what's going on with my father.

I'm not saying that on my mother's request. Her audacity in asking me to marry a man that I not only loathe but also despise is ridiculous, but I might have to play the game a little bit if I want to help my father out of whatever mess he'd gotten himself into.

I know that I don't have to do that and maybe it's not even my place, but whose place is it?

I love my father, despite all of his shortcomings, and I want to help him in any way that I can.

Getting back together with Henry at this point will only complicate things.

There's something else, too.

The other thing that I can't bring myself to say out loud is the fact that if I were to get back together with Henry, I would have to tell him about Franklin Parks.

Franklin is not only Henry's boss, but he's also the person who can help my father with his charges and help Tate Media get over this little bump in the road.

I don't know the details of any of this and I need to guard what I do know carefully. Henry does work for him and though I don't think he would betray me, the less that he knows the better.

When I think about Franklin, my chest tightens.

He is Henry's boss and he's the one who sent him away. He told me that he did it to break us up, but he framed it as a joke.

Was it, or did he just say it to make me feel bad?

Or both?

As I walk away from him down a

crowded New York street, I'm surrounded by a sea of people and I feel all alone.

I turn left and head toward Central Park.

I need to go somewhere where I can clear my head.

I need some nature in my life to help some of this make sense.

A few hours later, I get back to the hospital and spot an attorney sitting next to my mother.

4

AURORA

My mother, who has always been thin and trim, now looks frail and at least twenty years older than she really is.

She has been staying at the hospital for many days on end, only going home to shower and sleep for a few hours here and there.

Her dedication to my father is unnerving and never-ending, and I know that they have always been devoted to one another.

I admire that, but it doesn't change my complicated relationship with her.

I still have flashbacks back to that day when she showed up at my apartment and blamed me for everything that has happened to my father.

According to her, Franklin is the most powerful man in New York, if not the world, and everything that is happening right now, including the arrest and the heart attack, is my fault.

I take a deep breath as I walk down that loud linoleum floor toward the waiting area with a round collection of uncomfortable pink chairs, arranged to face the television on the other side of the wall.

The sound is off and the captions are so big that they take up half the screen. They are also about two minutes behind what the people are saying.

I watch a local reporter discuss a housefire in Staten Island, glancing at it occasionally as my mother talks to me.

She talks a lot under normal circumstances, but when she gets nervous, she talks at double her regular speed.

She gives me a brief update about my father. He is stable but the doctors are still watching his condition, whatever the hell that means.

She goes into the minutia of the medical evidence and all of the information goes in one ear and out the other. I've never been particularly good with biology and I have a D from 10th grade to prove it.

Eventually, I shift my attention to the stranger next to her, with his head buried in his phone. He's an attorney in his 50s with salt and pepper hair and the slim physique of someone who likes to work out and run a mile or two multiple times a week.

Is he the type to have a protein shake every morning and forgo all processed food? I wonder as I let my mind drift.

He introduces himself as Timothy Bradza and gives me a firm shake of his warm hand. He has a quiet demeanor that puts me at ease and I can see why my mother has retained him as counsel.

"Can you please tell my daughter what we talked about earlier?" Mom asks Timothy, looking away from me, annoyed and tapping her manicured nail on the plastic chair.

"Yes, of course," he says. "Well, to be honest with you, Aurora, the situation is quite bleak. The justice department has a strong case against your father for bribery and insider trading."

I give him a nod as if I understand what he is saying when in reality, I can barely wrap my head around it.

No, he must be wrong, I want to say. My father would never do that.

Why would he?

He's a multibillionaire who runs one of the most successful media companies in the world.

Why would he have to do anything like that?

Of course, I don't ask any of this. Instead, I just wait for him to continue.

"Also, they have numerous reports from shareholders and investors who say that they have had their retirements stolen as a result of this Ponzi scheme and, frankly, they are out for blood."

I shake my head, unwilling to believe this.

I look over at my mother, who looks just as dumbfounded.

Did she know? I ask myself.

"Is this all true?" I ask both my mother and the attorney.

She snaps her face toward mine and gets so close I can smell her minty fresh breath.

"Of course, it's not true," she hisses. "How could you even think that?"

The hairs on the back of my arms stand up.

She's so certain that she is either 100% right or 100% wrong. One thing is for sure, whatever it is that my father did or didn't do, she had to know.

Mr. Bradza's phone goes off and he excuses himself to take the call.

When we are alone, my mother moves one seat over to me.

"How dare you ask me that in front of him?" she whispers.

"What are you talking about?" I ask. "I thought he was our lawyer."

"Yes, he is, but he's also a stranger. He's not family."

I sigh and sit back in the chair.

I don't really know how to respond to this or anything that is happening.

"Did you know anything about this?"
I ask.

She pauses and looks me straight in the eye. For a moment, I think she's going to say yes.

"Your father would never do anything like that. How could you even suspect that?"

"Well, the cops must have something if they broke into his house in the middle of the night and arrested him, right? I mean, they wouldn't have done that if they didn't have something."

My mother leans over to me and slaps me across the face. My cheek burns and tears well up in my eyes. She has never hit me before and this comes completely out of nowhere.

"Don't you ever say that," she snaps, pointing her finger in my face. I lean away from her, but she gets closer. I shut my eyes and wait for her to hit me again.

"This is all your fault. Your father is being blamed, he's having his name smeared in the papers all because you turned that asshole down."

I stare at her in disbelief.

"What are you talking about?" I ask, still rubbing my cheek. The burning has subsided but now it has been replaced by an unfamiliar tingling sensation as if I have been scalded by something hot.

"Tate Media has not been doing well with investors and the stock price has been falling as you know. They don't have a case against him, not really, but Franklin is connected with the Attorney General and everyone else all the way up to the fucking president. So whatever he wants done, whatever show he wants to put on, it's put on. That's why they did that perp walk in front of all of the press, just to get his face in all of the papers. Ever since that happened, ever since the arrest, the stock price has plummeted. And I don't know what we can do to make it go back up."

I slump down in my seat. I don't really know what to say or what to do. My mother grabs her Birkin bag from the floor and places it on her lap. She pulls out a compact and powders her face before putting on a fresh coat of lipstick.

"I'm sorry I slapped you," she says,

looking at herself in the mirror. "I know that you didn't want to be involved with any of this, but now you are and I want you to stop acting like a child and grow the fuck up."

Without saying another word she gets up and walks away, her heels clicking loudly down the hallway. As soon as she disappears around the corner, tears rush down my face.

5

AURORA

I walk into my father's hospital room and look at a man that I don't even recognize.

When I was a child, my father was a God, tall, powerful, and completely invincible. But laying there in that hospital gown with the pillow propped up behind his head, he looks tired and worn out.

He forces a smile, and I force one back. I take his hand and ask him how he's feeling. He tries to sit up, but he doesn't have the strength.

He seems to have aged a decade in only a few days.

"I'm glad that you're feeling better," I say, patting his hand.

"Thank you for coming, it's good to see you," he says.

We don't talk about anything significant and just keep each other company for a while.

I don't remember the last time my father and I spent any significant time together. Honestly, ever since I started graduate school, I have been avoiding him.

I knew that he didn't approve but he paid my tuition despite it. It's a private university, and he barely noticed the $40,000 a year, but it was really a matter of principle.

He didn't want me "wasting my time pursuing things that didn't add to the bottom line," as he had called it.

The thing is that for him, passion and money were aligned. He wanted to start this business and it just happened to be a media company, and media companies just happen to make money, if they are run properly. But it's not like that at all pursuits, and that was something that he couldn't understand.

Occasionally, I glance back at the door to his room, keenly aware of the fact that there are two police officers stationed right outside.

This place isn't bugged, my father's investigators did their daily sweep only an hour before I arrived. We can talk about anything and everything that we want, at least for the time being, but the difficulty is approaching the subject, that's a little hard to stomach.

"Thank you for coming, Aurora," my father says, looking straight into my eyes.

While everything about him has aged, somehow his eyes have not.

"Of course," I say with a casual shrug. "I'm here for you, no matter what."

He smiles a little and looks out of the window.

"What, you don't believe me?" I ask.

"No, it's not that," he says, waving his hand, his body suddenly invigorated.

"I know that this is a difficult time for you," my father says. "The thing is that I know that we are asking you to do a very difficult thing."

He is avoiding saying the words directly, but we both know what he is getting at.

"Tell me what's going on, Daddy."

He shakes his head no.

"Please," I insist. "You've kept me in the dark for a long time."

He shakes his head again and then looks up at me, focusing his gaze on mine.

"That's not exactly what happened," he says. "Don't you remember?"

Now it's my turn to shrug and look away.

"You made it perfectly clear that you had no interest in being involved with Tate Media and we tried to keep you out of it for as long as possible."

"I appreciate that," I say. "But I would have much preferred a vice president position rather than a wife to the owner."

"That may be the case," Dad says, trying to sit up again. This time he succeeds. "But the thing is that you weren't involved earlier and things happened the way that they happened."

"What exactly is going on?"

He clears his throat and then says, "We are

in real trouble, pumpkin. Things have not been going well for some time. I've been trying to keep things afloat by telling the investors what they wanted to hear and hoping that I could get things to turn around, but I have not been as successful as I had wished."

He pauses for a moment and I wait for him to continue.

"Franklin Parks is the only one who can help us," Dad says. "He has connections that are… well, they are astonishing. He knows everybody and everybody owes him. That's why those charges were pressed so quickly. That's why they arrested me in the way that they did and that's why they were dropped just as fast afterward."

"But what does he want?" I ask.

I adjust my seat on the edge of my father's bed, trying to get comfortable without squishing him or any of the tubes running in and out of him.

"He wants you."

Dad and I have never talked about anything this private before. I mean, he knows that I have dated guys and was even serious with a few of them, but we have never really discussed my love life.

I knew that he did not approve of Henry, but he kept the details of his disapproval to himself.

This is the first time that we have ever broached the subject and it's disarming.

"Franklin Parks is a collector, honey. He likes to have things that are exclusive and hard to get and one of a kind. He has built up a large media conglomerate, but up until this point it has mainly been in the online space. He's looking to expand and buy something traditional, perhaps even old-fashioned. That's why he's interested in Tate."

"So, why doesn't he just make you an offer?"

"He has, and it was quite low. It's not enough to get us out from under our debts and it would leave us with very little to spare. Your mother and I did not build this fortune, this empire, to give it away, or worse yet sell it for parts."

"So, why can't you find another investor?" I ask.

"Don't you think that we have tried? We have been trying for two years. Things have been getting steadily worse and, with each quarterly report, things look even bleaker."

"Isn't there anything you can do?"

"I've already been fudging the profits a little bit. All in an effort to keep us afloat."

My chest tightens at the admission.

Putting out reports that do not reflect the truth about a company's profits and losses is a mortal sin in the financial world. Investors rely on that information to make decisions about the stock price and every other investment decision, and CEOs have been put away for many years for doing a lot less.

"So, where do I come in?" I ask.

"Franklin wants you to be his wife," my father says. There's no surprise or intonation in his voice when he says that. He says it in the same flat effect he has said everything else today.

My father is detached, almost as if he's not there at all. He's usually a little cold, a little distant, but this is on a whole new level.

"I don't understand what he wants from me, or why he even wants me to marry him.

When I talked to him, he told me that he had no interest in marriage at all."

"I don't know much about his intentions," my father says coolly. "But even if he were to reveal them to me, I would probably not trust them. People in our line of work tend to say things that don't really reflect the truth."

"That's one way of putting it," I agree.

He scoffs loudly and then clears his throat.

"I don't know much about Franklin, and we have investigators working on finding out more about him. But what they did find so far is that you two have actually met before when you were fifteen. He tried to come on to you and you turned him away."

I shake my head, trying to remember when this could've happened.

"It was at your debutante ball. He was hanging out with me and some of my friends from the club. Then at some point, you two had a chat."

Suddenly, I remember the precise moment. It was right outside the main ballroom, and I was standing by the wall, after feeling like I was about to have a panic attack.

I needed some quiet time to clear my head and the last thing that I expected was someone to approach me and flirt with me.

I was there with a date, whom I didn't particularly like, and this older guy came over, at first to just congratulate me. But he kept hanging around and, eventually, his friendliness became a little bit too much.

He made a joke and laughed, touching my shoulder and then my waist. I tried to back away from him, but there was nowhere to go.

Nothing he said was particularly funny, but I laughed along with him just to be nice, the way that girls do when they are uncomfortable.

When I tried to extricate myself from the situation, he didn't want to take no for an answer and I had to physically push him away.

"That sounds about right," he says when I go over the highlights. "He had mentioned that you were the only woman who has ever turned him away and that's why he wants you to be his wife."

"What can I do?" I ask him. "I mean, I want to help but can I really marry him?"

"No, you shouldn't marry him, pumpkin," my father says quietly. "Of course, you shouldn't marry him."

I let out a deep sigh of relief.

"You shouldn't marry him, but only if you're okay with losing everything," my father adds.

Shivers run down my spine and I can't feel the tips of my fingers.

"What are you saying?" I ask him, narrowing my eyes.

"I need your help, Aurora. I have never asked you for anything but now I need your help. This is just a marriage. It's nothing serious or life-altering."

I shake my head, unable to believe that my own father is saying this to me.

"Okay, okay," he says, raising his hands in the air in front of him.

He is trying to calm me down, reacting to the bewildered expression on my face.

"Let me explain," he continues. "What I

meant is that it's a big thing that you would be doing, I know that. It would be a huge favor to me and your mother and it would help us immensely. But I don't want you to think of it like your life is over. I know that you're no longer dating Henry, but if for some reason you still wanted to or if you met another person that you wanted to be with, you could, of course, be with him."

"Even if I'm married?" I ask.

"Come on now," he says. "We are all grown-ups here. Infidelity is very common in marriage, even ones that start out happy. I'm not saying that you won't be happy, but just in case you aren't…"

"Of course, I wouldn't be happy, I would be marrying a man that I hate. Or at the very least know nothing about. The only reason for a marriage is to save a company that I have nothing to do with."

My father furrows his eyebrows and he sits up more. Pointing his finger in my face, he narrows his eyes until his irises almost disappear.

"Let me explain something to you, honey," he says, using that word of endearment in a completely different way. "Tate Media is everything that I am and it is everything that your mother is. It is our baby. We have nurtured it from when it was a little seed and now it is a giant fucking oak tree. You did nothing to make it grow and we were okay with that. Now, you are the only one who can save it."

"If this is your way of asking me for a favor--" I start to say.

"I don't ask for favors," Dad says. "You either do this for yourself or you don't do it at all. Because don't forget that once they throw me in prison, they will freeze all of our assets, they will sell all of our homes and you and your brother will be left completely penniless. Besides, the fact that all of our employees and all of the pension funds that have invested in the company will lose everything. But no pressure, you do what's right for you."

6

AURORA

I leave my father's hospital room completely brokenhearted. When I first went in there, I thought that we could connect in a way that we haven't for a long time.

I thought that we would speak some truths and really learn about each other.

Perhaps, what has disappointed me most is that I have gotten exactly what I wanted.

I found out who my real father is and that he is not someone that I wanted to know.

Now I have to make a decision.

Despite who he is or who my mother is,

there are other considerations. Tate Media is a big company, a conglomerate, where lots of people work whose lives and livelihoods depend on its existence.

If I say no to this deal, then they will all lose their jobs. Unlike them, I don't have a family to support and I can deal with working a crappy job for some time.

What about all these other people who have devoted their lives to my parents' company? What happens to them?

Again, I wish that I could have Henry in my life to talk to. And if not him then at least a close friend or anyone that I could trust.

I have my mother and Ellis, of course, along with a whole bunch of other friends who are just as disconnected from who I am.

No, I need to make this decision on my own.

Later that evening, Franklin knocks on my door. I have invited him here for a talk. He comes in with a smile and a casual swagger, the kind that girls find irresistible.

I hate to admit it but he isn't particularly harsh on the eyes, so things could be worse.

"What am I doing here, Aurora?" he asks.

I find myself on my back foot right from the beginning. Instead of answering him right away, I turn my attention to the coffee that I had allegedly invited him in for.

"Do you take cream or sugar?" I ask.

"Both," he says and plops down on the couch.

He spreads himself out, draping his arms over the back, with his legs open wide. He's not the type to take up as little space as possible. He wants me to know that he is feeling comfortable and relaxed.

I make myself a black coffee and serve his cup on a tray with cream and sugar. I take a seat in the chair next to the couch. The cup feels nice against my cold skin, warming me from the outside in.

I take another long pause before opening my mouth to speak.

"I wanted to talk to you about the parameters of the deal," I say slowly but with great assurance.

I may be trembling on the inside, but I

am nothing but cool and collected on the outside.

"What deal?"

"It has come to my attention that you are interested in marrying me. Is that true?"

"Yes, I am," he says, looking straight into my eyes.

"And you are interested in buying Tate Media?"

"Yes, I am."

"Is there any way that you would consider making an offer on the company that doesn't include me?"

"No, not at this point."

"Why is that?"

Franklin adjusts himself slightly but doesn't take up any less room.

"I need a wife and I think you would make a good one," he says with a smile, bringing the cup to his mouth.

"Why is that?"

"I like you."

"You don't know anything about me."

"I know what I know. I see what I see."

He has been cryptic on purpose. He knows nothing about me. Right?

"So, what exactly are the parameters of this deal?" I come back to my initial question.

"I don't know what you mean," he says.

"Well, what will I have to do? How do you see all of this playing out?"

"How do I see all of this playing out?" he asks, putting his cup on the table and leaning closer to me.

"I made your father a very generous offer for Tate Media. He takes it and all of his troubles go away, with the investors, with the investigators."

"Are you going to pay them off?" I ask.

"In so many words, you could say that. I'm going to pay the investors everything that he owes them and then some and they will make the case against him go away."

"What do you want in return for all of this generosity?"

"You. I want you by my side."

I shake my head. He leans over to me and says, "You're smart, much smarter than your parents give you credit for. I need a strong woman to keep me in line, and to help me grow Tate Media into what we both know it can be."

"And what is that exactly?"

"With OMS ruling the online world and capturing 60% of the millennials and generation Z, and Tate media controlling the traditional television market, we would be unstoppable."

"I know what Tate can offer you," I say. "Credibility, being the number one thing. What I don't understand is why you can't just make an offer to my parents that doesn't include me?"

"I'm not really sure," Franklin says, leaning back again, bending his leg and placing his ankle on his knee. "But the more that you resist, and the more of these little interactions that we have, the more certain I am that this is the right decision for me. You know all the ins and outs of the company —"

"That's not true," I interrupt him. "I don't know anything about it. I've worked there as an intern for one summer and then couldn't get out of there fast enough."

"And why is that?" he asks.

"Because of my parents. They were

controlling and micromanaging every single moment of my life."

"Yes, I've dealt with some of that myself at OMS, so I know what you mean."

He is trying to connect with me, become my friend.

For now, I let him in.

If I want to play this game, and if I want to win, I need to know as much about him as he knows about me.

"How can you be so certain that the prosecutor will drop the case against my father?" I ask.

"He won't have any more witnesses after we pay back all of their allegedly stolen funds and give them a little bit off the top."

"That's illegal."

"Most things that get things done are illegal, Aurora. I thought you would know that by now."

I furrow my brow. I hate the way that he talks to me as if I am a little child. What's even more frustrating is that he both doesn't take me seriously and gives me too much credit.

"Do you have another plan in case that

one doesn't work out?" I ask. "Prosecutors don't tend to like to drop cases, especially big ones that have been splashed all around the tabloids."

"Why don't you leave that to me?" he suggests.

"No, I can't. I'm here to hammer out all of the details about our arrangement. If I were to go through with this wedding and marry you, I need to know what I would get from my end."

Franklin takes a deep breath and exhales even more slowly.

"There are a lot of powerful men who owe me many debts," he says after a moment. "I'm going to cash in all of my chips, as they say, and that's how I'm gonna make the case against your father go away."

When he glares into my eyes, I see a fire there that sends goose bumps down my arms.

I know that I shouldn't believe him, but I do.

When I go over to the kitchen to refresh our cups, I briefly glance over at my phone on the kitchen island.

With the screen off and the software hidden in a nondescript fitness app, it's recording and backing up every single thing that we have just said.

7

HENRY

When the thunderstorms roll in, I have a hard time getting out of bed. The sheets are soft and it feels like I'm sleeping on a cloud. They're so much better than they were in that apartment near my school.

The kitchen of this three-star hotel room is small, but I'm glad to have it. I've stayed in places without one before and it was always a pain to make all of my meals in the microwave or just eat vending machine food all the time.

The podcast game isn't glamorous. Some have studios and big budgets, but not mine.

Generation Crime with Henry Asher is a

shoestring operation and we record most of our interviews in hotel rooms just like this, using my laptop and a few microphones.

This is how I started out when I first got the job at Tate Media. They added a little bit to the budget allowing me to get a partner but not much else.

My partner, Liam Kazinski, is sitting across from me as I narrate the last bits of this week's episode.

This season, which we recorded over the series of a month, focuses on a teenage girl whose body was found in an irrigation ditch behind the library that she used to love to go to as a little girl. The man responsible for her death is a guy who attended a nearby high school who forced her into prostitution, made her run away from home, and eventually killed her.

Elizabeth Kenner came from an upper-middle-class family with long roots in Kentucky.

Her father and his father were both dentists and her mother was a homemaker who raised two other children.

Elizabeth was the oldest and to say that

her disappearance and eventual murder came as a shock to her family would be a grave understatement.

Her father dealt with it by burying himself in his work. He died of a heart attack two years later, a year before her body was found.

With two small children to raise, Mrs. Kenner focused her attention on setting up an organization that helps parents of runaways. That's why she's here talking to me. She wants to raise awareness about how dangerous it is for teenagers to run away since many end up homeless and become victims of sexual and physical abuse.

I don't have much experience doing formal interviews, but with my work with the podcast, I've had to learn everything rapid-fire.

Mrs. Kenner answers all of my questions and after I stop recording, she thanks me and Liam for bringing attention to her daughter's case.

"A lot of people assume that she came from a bad home or somehow deserved what had happened to her," Mrs. Kenner says, "but the truth is none of them do. Teenagers run away because they think it's romantic. They want to break the rules, they want to do what they want to do, and they shouldn't pay with their lives for wanting to live a little bit on the edge."

I thank her again for coming in and speaking with me and show her to the door.

We have invited her to stay for dinner, a glamorous dinner of takeout from the Denny's across the street, but she declines.

She doesn't want to make friends with people who know her deepest and darkest pain and I understand that.

After she leaves, I ask Liam to wrap up the recording session before dinner.

We are both hungry, but I want to put this case behind us and really celebrate.

No, maybe celebrate is the wrong word.

I don't have anything to celebrate.

The reason that I'm back in Kentucky is that I'm running away from life as I know it.

But it's good to put a period at the end of the sentence and that's why I want to finish talking about this case before dinner.

"What a terrible story," Liam says into

the microphone after I read from the script that I put together earlier today. "But of course it is so important that we share it so that others can learn from it."

"Yes, I totally agree with you," I say. "That's one of the reasons we do what we do here at Generation Crime with Henry Asher."

At this point, I'm supposed to read a promo for the podcast's sponsor; an online mattress store, but I get lost in the paperwork and read the wrong script.

"Oh, shit," I say with the recording still running.

Liam shakes his head.

"I'm sorry, man." I guess I'm hungrier than I thought.

"Let's just finish it when we get back, I'm starving," he insists.

I shake my head no, scrambling for the right ad.

At one point I had them all printed out, God knows why, but now I just scroll up through the Word document where I had organized the whole story and find it at the very beginning.

"Let me just do this part again," I insist.

We get to Denny's fifteen minutes later. A familiar waitress welcomes us in.

After a month of living here, she knows both of our names and we know all of the waitresses who work here.

This one is Maureen, she is eighteen-years-old with pimples to show for it and the casual quiet demeanor of someone who would prefer to spend her days thinking about dragons and swordplay rather than omelet grand slams and hash browns.

Maureen is a big fan of the Witcher, the latest Netflix sensation, and the three of us bond over this fact. She has never heard of a podcast until she met us and I showed her how to access the Podcast App on her iPhone.

"I never even knew what this button did," she said. "And they're all free?"

"Yep," I confirmed. "And not all of them are about crime. A lot of them are about politics and there are lots of really good ones about various curiosities and unusual stories. If you like science-fiction and fantasy, there are a ton of podcasts about that."

"Awesome, I'll definitely check them out," she promised.

At the time, I thought that she was just being nice, but she surprised me.

I see her a few times a week and every time she introduces me to a new fantasy podcast that I've never heard of that she has already binged.

"You know, I'm going to miss seeing you every week," I tell her.

"Why is that?" she asks.

"Well, we just did our last interview and we're heading back home soon."

"Oh, no, that's too bad. Any chance that you'll be back?"

"Not likely," I say.

After she leaves to get our orders, Liam takes a sip of his soda and mentions how he wishes that Leslie was working tonight.

I laugh and shake my head.

Leslie is twenty-seven-years-old with two children and a husband who went out to get some milk one night and never came back.

She knew enough not to get her hopes up with Liam, but they've enjoyed each other's company for a few nights and from what I've heard, they have both had a good time.

"So, how are things with Aurora?" he asks when Maureen comes back with our food.

I shrug and dig my fork into the pancakes.

"Not that great," I say. "I went up to New York and I tried to talk to her but she wasn't interested."

Liam sighs heavily.

He isn't much of a ladies' man and seems to be the kind of guy who is just looking to find that one special girl he can spend the rest of his life with.

I never wanted any of that before, but now I'm not so sure. The only problem is that the girl that I want isn't available.

"What's going to happen with Leslie?" I ask.

He shrugs and takes a bite of his hash browns.

"I like her a lot," he admits, "even if she has children."

"You don't want children?" I ask.

"No, it's not that. It's just that I don't

know how I would be as a stepfather. But it's not like any of that matters. She lives here. She is still technically married-"

"Her husband did leave her eighteen months ago and she hasn't heard from him since," I point out. "I'm not sure that she's exactly married in the traditional sense."

"That may be the case but, come on now, Henry. This isn't realistic. I mean, I live in New York. She lives in Louisville. She has two kids. She has a job."

"She's a waitress," I say. "Nothing against waitressing, but I'm pretty certain that she can get that kind of position in New York as well, and it probably pays a lot better."

"Look, I would love to ask her to come with me, but where? I live in a studio apartment. What, is she gonna leave her kids here? Besides, you know that her parents don't approve of me."

"Fuck that," I say.

"They're still her parents and they help her take care of the kids and she lives with them."

"They're racists," I insist. "The only

reason they don't approve of you is that you're black."

"Whatever," Liam says, waving his hand. "They are a big part of her life and I don't know if I can fill whatever void they would leave if she were to come with me."

"Listen," I say, finishing the last of my pancakes. "I know that this is kind of a complicated situation, but I just want to tell you not to waste your chance. If there's even an inkling in your mind that this girl might be the right one for you, I want you to do everything in your power to make her yours."

"Is that your advice to me? Or is that the advice that you would give yourself?" he asks.

Of course, I'm talking about Aurora.

Given everything that happened between us, I have a lot of regrets.

That's just how things are.

"You're my friend and I don't want you to make the same mistakes I have," I say quietly.

8

AURORA

The interviewer arrives at twilight, just as the city is settling in for the evening. She is a peppy and eager woman in her mid-20s with a red mane that cascades down her back. She smiles and nods taking down everything that Franklin says.

She's just as methodical in jotting down my words, but something is different, nevertheless.

She knows exactly how influential Franklin can be in her career.

She wants to make a good impression and she wants him to like this article.

"So, how is it that you two met?" she asks, bringing her pen to her mouth.

When Franklin glances at her, her eyes light up, and he looks her up and down the way that men assess women at bars.

This is the man that I'm going to marry and he can't even contain himself during our engagement interview for the New York Chronicle.

I can't let this bother me I decide. He is acting polite and approachable and that's what I need to do.

I glance over at the videographer who has his camera pointed in my face.

"Would you mind if I confirm a few facts for the background material?" Danielle asks.

We are sitting in Franklin's living room, which is currently disguised as a stage. There are lights everywhere and furniture has been rearranged so that it looks good on film.

"Of course not," I say.

She gives me a slight nod and then turns her attention back to Franklin.

"You have attended Princeton University and majored in economics?" she asks.

"Yes, with a concentration on finance."

"And before that, you attended Saint Ambrose, which is a boarding school?"

"Oh, no," he says, "are we going back all the way to high school?"

Danielle laughs. "Well, it is a very well-known school. They would appreciate it if I mention it."

"Yes, I'm sure that they would," Franklin admits. "The problem is that I won't."

He stares at her without changing his facial expression until she laughs uncomfortably.

"I graduated from Barnard College with a bachelor's degree in English and then I got my master's and PhD at Columbia."

"What would you say it was like to go to an all-girls school?" Danielle asks.

I am slightly taken aback by how easily she dismissed my years of post-graduate work, but I take a quick breath and let it go.

"Well, that's hard to say, since it's not really an all-girls school the way that some of them are. It's right across the street from Columbia University, being their sister school, going back to when Columbia was only for boys. I took a number of my classes at Columbia, in fact, I took the majority of my courses there. Besides, it's also right in the middle of Manhattan. But I guess to answer your question, it was a good experience. I had a little bit of a sisterhood, which was really nice."

This is a lie. Though I enjoyed the school for its academic rigor, I didn't really make any friends there.

Looking back now, I know that it was my fault.

I had never been particularly social and when girls tried to connect with me at the beginning of the year, I was too shy. After a while, they stopped asking.

I somehow lock myself off from people. Most probably assume that I'm stuck up or too good for them, but the reality is that I just don't know how to make friends.

On top of that, the course-load that I was taking was way too difficult and I always felt behind and out of control.

Even if I couldn't study every waking hour of every day, I would sit in my room and procrastinate, thinking that just being at my desk was enough. And when you are so busy pretending to do work, you can't very well go out with anyone and actually take time off.

"Is everything okay?" Danielle asks.

I glance at her and realize that I had drifted off in the middle of the conversation.

"Yes, of course." I snap my face and my plastic smile back into place. "I'm sorry about that, I just got lost in thinking about how happy Franklin makes me feel."

I squeeze his hand as I say this and he squeezes mine.

Looking at him from the outside, not even I can tell that he is not madly in love.

How does that line go again?

All the world's a stage and we are all just players. It's in instances like these that it's so easy to forget the truth.

"Well, this must be wonderful news for your family, Aurora," Danielle says. "I mean, given everything that has happened to your father…"

She doesn't come out and directly mention the arrest or the heart attack but she expects me to comment on it anyway.

"Yes, it is a relief that the charges have

been dropped and my father is okay. That was a very stressful situation for him, it's one of the reasons why he suffered the heart attack in the first place."

"Mr. Tate is now at home resting and he will be back in fighting stance very soon," Franklin adds. "Let's not forget that he is a giant of the industry and it will take a lot more than that to take him out of commission."

Danielle smiles, happily jotting down the quote that I know will probably appear somewhere in bold in the article, if not be incorporated into the headline.

The New York Chronicle is not directly owned by Tate Media but it is friendly to the company. That's one of the reasons why they got the interview in the first place.

In our business, it is all about spin and creating the reality you want to live in so that others will join you there as well.

And the more articles that you can flood the world with that show everyone how wonderful you are, then the further you'll go in getting what you want.

"I also wanted to ask you about your

father's arrest," Danielle says, catching me by surprise. We had previously come to an agreement about what she would and would not ask directly.

This question is out of bounds.

"Where were you when it happened?" she asks.

"At home," I say. "My mother showed up at my door really early in the morning and told me what happened. It was a really scary time because I had no idea why they would arrest him or why any of that was happening."

"Yes, I can imagine."

"And what about when you first heard about the charges? What did you think?"

My mind goes blank.

All I remember is how I felt finding out what had happened.

I wasn't so much devastated for my father as I was angry with him for doing everything that he had done to get him in that situation.

Of course, people are arrested every day who are completely innocent of all of the charges levied against them.

But I have a feeling that my father did not fall into that category.

"She was completely devastated," Franklin steps in to help me out, pulling me closer to him.

"She called me right away, in tears," he continues. And if you know anything about this girl you know that she doesn't cry easily."

"I can only imagine how difficult it must've been for you," Danielle says.

"You don't even know half of it," Franklin insists. "Even now, bringing it up, this is why she has become so quiet. It was a very scary situation and it's one we prefer not to relive."

"Yes, of course, I totally understand."

"All I can say is that we are relieved that all of the charges have been dropped," Franklin says. "But we are very disappointed in the police department and the prosecutor's office for bringing them in the first place."

"Some people would say that it was a very uncanny coincidence that the charges were dropped so quickly after the engagement and your announcement that you are interested in buying Tate Media," Danielle points out, looking directly at me.

"Perhaps." I had underestimated her.

I thought that she was just a wide-eyed girl, happy to write any line of bullshit that Franklin spews, but now I see that perhaps she's not so stupid after all.

Of course, I can't justify her point with any sort of affirmative remark.

"Whoever says that is making a connection that simply does not exist," I say.

"What do you mean?" she asks.

"Well, Franklin is a family friend and we met and fell in love and he asked me to marry him and I said yes. None of that had anything to do with what happened to my father or his stake in the company."

"So, that was just all one big coincidence?" she asks.

"A coincidence would imply that the events were somehow related and they're not at all," I say.

"Aurora went through a difficult time and I was there for her and it was during that ordeal that I realized just how much I wanted to marry her," Franklin adds. "I wasn't sure what she would say but I am eternally grateful that her answer was yes."

Danielle doesn't look convinced, but whatever doubts she has she lets them go.

9

HENRY

I watch the interview on YouTube with my mouth open. It's all over the news and all over the major gossip outlets.

It is an interview about their engagement, but it has

hundreds of thousands of views.

Aurora is an heiress to a multibillion-dollar fortune and even though she has never had the notoriety of Paris Hilton, her name represents something very important in New York society.

Franklin Parks is an online media darling and the fact that he made an offer on her father's company and that offer has been accepted is a big deal.

Tate Media has a strong foundation and an unwavering reputation. Whatever issues it has encountered in recent months have suddenly all been forgotten.

The interview doesn't go very deep into any of the rumors, just glossing over and focusing on the wedding planning.

How could I have not known? I wonder.

I had worked with the guy and I had no idea. Franklin is my boss and now I find out that he is actually a founder of one of the biggest online media companies in the world.

Perhaps, I should have done some basic research but he didn't become an actual celebrity until they announced their engagement.

So, what was he doing working in my department? What was he doing hiring me and distributing stories directly to me?

Was this all a power-play?

I shake my head as I try to figure out what has happened.

One part of me keeps thinking that it must be a coincidence.

He worked for Tate Media in order to

get better acquainted with how they do things and he started a new department there and wanted to run it himself.

But another part of me goes somewhere darker. Perhaps, Franklin knew that he wanted to buy Tate Media and he knew that he wanted to make Aurora his wife.

But at that time, she was dating me and he wanted to break us up.

Could that be it? Could that be the reason he hired me and sent me away on assignments?

But why?

Could he have been that diabolical?

Besides, why would he even bother with something like that?

There is, of course, another option. We broke up and he pounced.

Aurora was confused and lost and he took advantage of her and now she's floating on cloud nine thinking that everything's gonna be okay and that she's marrying the right person.

"Henry?" Liam asks, walking over to me.

I'm sitting on the most uncomfortable couch in the world, thousands of miles away from my home, watching the woman I love tell a reporter how much she loves her fiancé.

"Something is wrong here," I say, taking off my headphones and pointing to the screen. "They just started dating. I mean, we just broke up. How could this be happening already?"

"Okay, I don't want to be an asshole, but have you considered the possibility that maybe they didn't just start dating?"

I snap my head back to face him.

"What are you talking about?"

"Think about it. You were out here for a long time covering different stories. You guys weren't talking much, you said so yourself."

"Yeah, we were drifting, so what?"

"Well, have you ever thought that maybe she just drifted into his arms a little bit before you broke up?" he asks.

I stare at him in disbelief.

Is he really saying this?

What does he mean exactly?

I shake my head and repeat "no, no, no over and over again."

"Listen, you have to consider the

possibility that she was cheating on you. I mean, of course, it's possible that they met and fell in love after you broke up, but they knew each other beforehand, right?"

"So?" I ask.

"Well, if he was a family friend of her parents, then they've met before. They've known each other and who knows what else happened?"

His words feel like little stabs to my heart.

Each breath makes the cuts deeper and deeper until my chest contracts and I can't take a single breath.

We watch the rest of the interview in silence. I had already watched it twice, but I turn up the volume so that Liam can see it.

In the end, the reporter brings up the suspiciousness of the engagement being so close to the time when the charges against her father are dropped.

Aurora denies a connection, but there's something in her face that tells me that she's lying.

It's hard to explain what that is exactly.

It's the way that she moves her jaw and readjusts in her seat.

Despite everything that has happened, I know the real Aurora. That's the woman that I fell in love with and that's the one I'm going to get back.

Later that evening, I walk back-and-forth in my hotel room trying to figure out what to do. I just got back and I'm not entirely over what she said to me outside that bookstore, but I know that I have to talk to her again.

I have to find out the truth.

It would be a lie to say that Liam did not plant an idea in my mind about what may or may not have happened when I was away.

I thought that Aurora and I were just growing apart from the distance, but now I wonder if it was a lot more sinister than that.

Was she seeing Franklin behind my back?

Was he lying to me the whole time when I called him to talk about the stories I was working on?

Was I a joke that they shared between themselves?

I can't possibly know the answers to any

of these questions, but they keep me up all night nevertheless.

Around two in the morning, after I've had more than a few beers, I can no longer resist making the call.

I regret it as soon as I dial but I don't hang up.

Instead, I wait.

"Answer, please answer," I whisper alone into the dark.

"Why don't you answer the phone?" I ask louder when her voice mail comes on.

I'm tempted to leave a message, but I wait too long.

Then before I know what I'm even doing, I dial again.

This time, it goes straight to voice mail.

"Hey, Aurora, it's me," I say. My voice is shaky and full of pauses. "I just heard that you got engaged to Franklin Parks, of all people. What's that about?"

I wait for her to answer as if I'm actually talking to her.

"How could you do this to me? I thought that we had something special. Are you really going to marry him?"

I want to hang up and try to physically force myself to do it but I can't stop myself from talking.

"I really loved you, no, that's not accurate. I really love you. I don't know how everything went wrong so quickly. I really thought that you were going to be the one. I thought that after you graduated, you'd come out and work with me or I would come back to New York and get a job there but then things just went to shit.

"And now, you're engaged? To my boss? My friend here told me that something was probably going on even before we broke up.

"Is that true? I never thought that you would be the kind to cheat, but what the hell do I know about you anyway? I'm just a broke writer without a dollar to my name and now probably not even a job. And you? You stand to inherit a billion-dollar fortune. Or is it a few billions? Who can keep track? And now you're marrying another billionaire?

"So, is that what was going on this whole time? Were you just slumming it with me? Were you just dating me to get a rise out of your parents, to make them a little angry? Is this all that we ever were?

"I want to ask you to call me back, but I sort of suspect that you probably won't. So let me just say that my feelings for you were always real. And if you lied to me and cheated on me, then that's on you. Maybe I was wrong about who you were all along. Have a good life."

10

HENRY

The following day I get a call from Franklin. I see his name on the screen and my chest tightens.

Did she tell him that I left that message? What do I say if she did?

I'm tempted to answer and immediately accuse him of stealing my girlfriend, but I force myself to keep my anger in check.

The only thing that I have going for me right now is this job and like it or not Franklin is still my boss.

"Hello?" I say into the phone.

"Hey there," he says in his peppy voice. "Long time no chat."

"Yeah, I meant to get back to you about that last email but I just got really busy."

Franklin is the type of guy who likes to handle a lot of things over the phone rather than via text or email.

We talk a little bit about work and then the weather. When we reach a lull in the conversation, I finally bring it up.

I debate whether I should but my curiosity and my need to know the truth gets the better of me.

"Congratulations on your engagement," I say, completely out of the blue.

"Um, thank you," he stutters. I have managed to catch him by surprise.

"How did you…?" he asks, letting his voice drop off.

"Well, you did that interview with the Chronicle and I saw the video on YouTube.".

"Yes, of course."

"It's not every day that an heiress to a massive fortune marries another billionaire, right? And now I hear that you were also in negotiations to make an offer on Tate Media?"

"I guess some things are hard to keep secret, huh?" he asks.

"Well, you seem to do a pretty good job of it. I mean, I had no idea that you were the founder of an OMS."

"Yeah, sorry about that," Franklin says. "I wanted to get to know everyone without you knowing who I was...in the Undercover Boss sort of way."

I've never seen that show but apparently that's a thing that some CEOs do.

"You understand, of course?"

I give him a slight nod but say nothing.

"Henry?"

"Yeah, I'm here," I say quickly. "Yes, of course, you don't owe me an explanation."

"Actually, that's not entirely true," Franklin says with a deep sigh. "I should have told you about Aurora."

My mouth is parched. I run my tongue over my chapped lips and say nothing.

Suddenly, my phone rings and I see that he's trying to connect with me over FaceTime.

"I just really wanted to tell you this in person," Franklin says after I click Accept.

I don't want to see him and suddenly I am very aware of how worn out and disheveled I look in comparison to him with his perfectly coiffed hair and tailored suit.

Franklin spins in his chair and I see the expanse of the New York skyline behind him in the floor-to-ceiling windows that grace his office.

"You're one of the best people that I have working for me. I feel like we really made a connection that goes beyond boss – employee, over these last few months," Franklin says, peering into my phone.

I give him a slight nod and sit back against the old squeaky couch in my hotel room along a busy, industrial highway.

"Yes, I appreciate you saying that. I have enjoyed working for this company a lot and I really like doing the podcast and working on all of these stories."

"Well, I just want you to know that nothing is going to change that. You do really good work and I want you to continue working for us."

We are still not talking about the elephant in the room.

He is circling, but not quite getting to the point.

"Thank you," I say and pick out something on the coffee table, just out of sight.

I want to bring up Aurora but I don't quite know what to say. I don't want to come straight out and accuse him of an affair because I don't want to lose my job.

"Can I ask you something?" I ask. He nods. "How long have you been seeing Aurora?"

Franklin takes a pause but doesn't lose eye contact with me.

"We connected right after you broke up."

"How soon?"

"Pretty soon," he says.

I hate the vagueness of his responses.

"But if you think that there was anything going on while you were still together, I'm here to tell you that that's not true."

"And now you're engaged?"

"Well, we had known each other a little bit beforehand. Our families know each other through business. And after we got together, it just felt right. For both of us."

I take a deep breath and exhale slowly.

I'm not sure what to say.

I don't know if I believe him about the cheating since the quickness of the engagement still seems a bit far-fetched.

Deep down in my soul, I know who Aurora is. She's not the type to make rash decisions, especially given everything that's been going on with her father.

"I really hope that you don't let this little hiccup interrupt or get in the middle of our working relationship," Franklin says. "Maybe if we were other people, we would find it difficult to work with each other, given the fact that you once dated my future wife. But I really hope that we are better people than that."

"Yes," I agree, "we shouldn't let this get in the way."

It's good to keep him on my side for now. I have more questions, but I need to get back to New York to find those answers.

He doesn't bring up my call to Aurora

last night and I wonder if she just didn't tell him or he just didn't bring it up.

Did she even listen to it? Or did she just delete it without a second thought?

"Well, I really do appreciate you calling me and us clearing the air, so to speak," I say with a newfound pep in my voice. "And now that I'm done with the project here, I plan on getting on the next flight to New York. I have a lot of good ideas for more stories —"

"Actually, that's what I wanted to talk to you about. There's a new story that I think that you might be very interested in, but unfortunately it's not in New York."

I tighten my fist, until my knuckles get white.

"I really need to get back home," I say.

"I need to see my mom, I'm sure that there are lots of stories that I can focus on in the tri-state area."

"Yes, that's true," Franklin says. "But this is the story that will make you a real investigative journalist. And I have a feeling that if you do your job right, which I'm sure you will, we can get it submitted for the Pulitzer Prize."

My mouth nearly drops open.

"What are you talking about?"

"They have created a new category, Audio Reporting, making podcasts eligible for consideration."

The Pulitzer is the Holy Grail of all journalism and the jury typically consists of distinguished journalists in each category who evaluate the entries and make final decisions.

"But I'm not really a reporter," I insist.

"You're a good investigator and you're a good storyteller. You're a good writer and that makes you a good reporter. Your podcast is top notch and working on this new story will put you at the top," Franklin says.

I'm not so sure but I keep my doubts to myself.

"This is a very big story, Henry. Do you want to hear about it or not?"

I give him a slight nod.

"It happened in North Dakota and involves the fracking industry. Remember when they had the oil boom there and basically built an economy out of nothing in a few years?

"Hundreds of thousands of young men moved there for jobs. Houses that used to cost twenty grand suddenly cost half a million and rents were similar to what they are in Manhattan. Workers slept in cars wherever they could, just to make the six-figure salaries that they could never make anywhere else."

"Yes, I'm somewhat familiar with what happened. But then gas prices dropped and it all went to shit."

"Well, whatever goes up must come down, right?"

"I guess," I say without much enthusiasm.

"So, what is the angle here, exactly?" I ask. "There are already thousands of stories about the gas industry in North Dakota."

"Hold your horses." Franklin laughs. "Yes, you're right, there are lots of stories about the rise and fall of shale oil. But the thing that I want you to focus on is what happened to one teenage girl who went there with her boyfriend.

He got a job at an outfit, they were both from Tennessee, somewhere in Appalachia where there were no jobs and no prospects. They heard about what was going on and they decided to take a chance. It worked out for him, somewhat, but not so much for her."

"What happened?" I ask.

"Her body was found in a ditch not too far away from their apartment. The authorities thought that he did it but could never get enough evidence."

"Isn't it always the boyfriend or a husband?" I ask. "Besides, what makes you think that I'll be able to find out anything that the police did not?"

"I don't know what you will be able to find," Franklin says. "That's the whole point. I want you to write your investigation and do the podcast as you are investigating the story. We don't know the answer, but the readers and the listeners are there to go on the journey with us."

"But I'm not an investigator," I say after a moment. "If I do this, and that's a big if, I will need more help."

"Of course, anything you need."

I think about it for second.

It would be a lie to say that I'm not interested in the story, but I have something else in mind as well.

"I would need a real private investigator," I say after a moment.

There's a pause on the other end.

"Liam is great, and we work really well together but neither of us really know anything about investigating. I know someone who used to be a cop from back home who now works as a PI. He would be great."

I can hear Franklin thinking, so I add, "He's not very expensive."

"Now that is music to my ears," Franklin says.

11

AURORA

I stand in the middle of a Fifth Avenue bridal boutique with tears running down my cheeks.

I'm dressed in a large cupcake fluffed type of gown with a long train that requires at least three people to carry it. This is the gown that my mother has picked out.

She's sitting on the plush couch right behind me with the biggest smile I have ever seen.

Ellis and a few of my other friends from school are with her, all holding hands and giggling with excitement.

They think that my tears are from happiness, but they are anything but that.

"You look marvelous," Mom exclaims, wiping the corner of her own eye with a handkerchief.

I had tried on four other dresses and managed to keep my feelings and emotions in check.

I don't feel like this is *the one* any more than I felt that way about any of the other dresses. The only thing that's different is that I was stupid enough to listen to Henry's voice mail *again* while I was in the dressing room.

He left me a long, detailed message in the middle of the night, and I have re-listened to it multiple times a day ever since. I want to call him back more than anything and tell him what is really going on, but I don't think that I will be able to go through with this if he knows the truth.

And to save my father's life and to save my family's legacy, this is the only way to do it.

I'm not sure why I reached for my phone right after I had put on that wedding dress.

A part of me just wanted to hear Henry's voice again.

Another part of me wanted to feel closer to him while I was trying on a wedding dress.

It's hard to explain exactly, but it should be him who is at the end of that aisle, not Franklin Parks.

"This dress looks beautiful, honey, but I think that we should try on one of the more slimming ones instead," Mom says.

"Sure, whatever," I say, stepping down from the pedestal.

"Do you not agree?" she asks.

"No, of course I do."

This is one of my mother's not so subtle ways of telling me that I have gained a few pounds. Everyone sitting on the couch across from me is tall, thin, and elegant.

They are everything that I am not, and probably everything I will never be.

And you know what? That's okay with me.

I may not have the perfect body, but I'm sick and tired of hating it. Sometimes, you reach the point when you can no longer hate yourself. Sometimes, you realize that maybe you should feel grateful instead.

Instead of focusing on the size of my hips, I should be grateful that I can run and walk and jump. I should be happy that I can do all of those things without any pain and that my body works exactly as it should.

I have been living with my mother's perception and the world's perception of me for way too long.

I don't need to look like anyone else, I just need to look at myself.

Moreover, I don't need to apologize for what I look like.

WHEN I GET BACK to the dressing room, I take off my dress and look at my body. The light here isn't harsh and directly overhead like it usually is.

It's soft and welcoming and the mirror is tilted to the best possible angle. All of this is done to make the women feel more attractive, more beautiful. And it works.

The stomach that I thought looked so terrible, is relatively slim. There are curves, of course, but even they are alluring.

Is this how Henry sees me? Or rather, is this how he *saw* me?

He loved my body more than anyone else and more than I ever thought anyone could.

A quiet knock on the door makes me jump.

"Aurora?" the woman on the other side asks in a meek voice.

"Who is it?"

"It's Karlie," she says. "Karlie Renton."

I shake my head no and crack the door open. Then I come face-to-face with a girl I haven't seen since the ninth grade.

"Oh my God," I whisper. "Is it really you?"

I wrap my arms around her and pull her into the dressing room.

"What are you doing here?" I ask, quickly covering myself up with the silk bathrobe they gave me to wear in between dress fittings.

"I work here now," she says.

The woman who stands before me now has chestnut hair cut to the shoulders, styled in waves, and a warm tan complexion.

Back when we knew each other, she was a short thirteen-year-old with dyed black hair, powdered white skin, and dark lips. She wasn't exactly a Goth but well on her way.

"When was the last time we saw each other? I ask.

"Ten years, I guess. Maybe more. I moved away the summer before 10th grade."

"Florida, right?"

"Miami," she says. "My parents sold their business and retired. It was always their dream to live there full-time."

"So, what brought you back here?"

"Well, if I were telling the truth, I'd say a break-up."

"Really?"

"Yeah, okay, don't take this the wrong way but I'm sort of going through something."

"What do you mean?" I ask.

"I was in this really unhealthy relationship for about four years and I finally broke out of it and ever since then I've decided to be more honest with myself and with those around me. That's why when you asked, I didn't just say for a job or whatever other stupid excuse. No, I moved here to get away from life as I knew it."

I stare into her wide open eyes and her unassuming demeanor.

I don't think I've ever admired anyone more than I admire her in this moment.

There's nothing to say. Instead I wrap my arms tightly around her.

"Would you like to try on the next dress?" a woman asks through the door, startling me. "Your mother said that she can't stay much longer."

12

AURORA

I don't know why Karlie and I ever had a falling out. In fact, we didn't. We were friends in math class because we were both quite good at it and the teacher always paired us up together. When we found out we liked the same boy, we promised that neither of us would go out with him if he asked and we kept that promise.

And then one day, she came over and told me that she was moving during spring break. Her parents weren't even waiting until the end of the year.

We promised to stay in touch but you

know how it is, long-distance friendships, just like long-distance relationships, rarely last.

Over lunch after my dress fitting, Karlie tells me that her parents wanted to move there after her father's retirement. At least, that's what her father told her and her mother that spring.

But right before her graduation, she found out the truth.

Her father wanted to move there because he'd started seeing a woman in Miami, who he'd met on a business trip, and this woman was pregnant and expecting his child.

Karlie didn't meet her sister until she was almost three years old, when her father filed for divorce and moved in with his girlfriend.

"It really messed me up," Karlie says, taking a sip of her wine. "I mean, I couldn't trust men for a long time, and that was when I was supposed to be dating and meeting lots of them. You know, in college…"

"Where did you go to school?" I ask.

"University of Florida."

I give her a slight nod, which she takes as judgment.

'If you remember, I was a scholarship kid. My parents never really had much money. I mean, my dad sold insurance, so we were comfortable but not like all the other kids at our school. And when it came to saving for college, he didn't really do that. He had a pretty bad gambling addiction."

"University of Florida is a really good school," I reaffirm her.

"I know that that's what you think, but that's not what your friend Ellis would say."

"Oh, who cares about her?"

"You do," Karlie says. "Why else would she be at your dress fitting?"

I shrug and look down at my plate. My cheeks blush from embarrassment.

"She's not really my friend," I say after a moment. "She is just someone I have been friends with for a long time and that's how it has always been. I don't know, it's hard to explain. Our parents are friends and we have all of these other friends in common…"

I let my voice trail off.

After a moment I look up at her.

I don't know if she's judging me, but I am judging myself.

Why am I friends with someone that I don't really like? I wonder.

"Anyway, I don't want to make you feel bad," Karlie says. "I'm sure that Ellis has a lot of redeeming qualities."

Her voice is drenched in sarcasm.

"She was really mean to you," I admit. "I am really sorry."

"Why?" Karlie asks. "You had nothing to do with that."

"I know, I just feel shitty about it. I should have stopped her. I should've stood up for you more."

We sit quietly for a few moments thinking back to that horrible time called high school when your whole life seems to be both run on an accelerator and with a brake at the same time.

Every little moment is super charged, every little interaction with a friend or foe, making time pass both impossibly quick and slow like molasses.

Ellis was a bully.

There's no other way around it. She treated everyone like dirt beneath her thousand dollar heels especially the scholarship kids.

She was one of the most popular girls at school and one of the reasons for that is because she was so stuck up.

While everyone else was trying desperately to find a group to fit into, a clique of friends where they could be at home, Ellis walked around with her nose in the air as if none of that mattered.

She was above all that, and it was up to everyone else to want to be friends with her.

The thing is that that worked out. Everyone wanted to be friends with her because she was this unattainable goal.

One of Ellis's strong suits was finding the thing that you were most insecure about and focusing in on that to make you feel like shit.

With Karlie, and other students on financial aid, she would make fun of their clothes and makeup and hair.

If you stood up to her, like Karlie did, that only made things worse.

"She made fun of me for a lot of

things," Karlie says, "but it's the jokes that she made about my weight that hurt the most. I can't help the fact that all of my hormones were out of whack and all I wanted to do was eat all the time. My weight was one of my biggest demons and she just made me feel a hundred times worse about it than I already did."

"I'm really sorry," I whisper, not knowing what else to say.

"She did it again today," Karlie says.

I look up at her, furrowing my brows.

"What are you talking about?" I ask.

"That's how I found out that you were here. I saw her out front and I had hoped that she wouldn't notice me, or at least not recognize me, but unfortunately, she did. She gave me a hug as if we were old friends and asked me all about my life. And she told me that you were in the dressing room."

"Did she say something to you?" I ask.

"Well, she wasn't as obvious as she was before. But as soon as I walked away and she thought that I was out of earshot, I heard her tell everyone how fat I used to be and 'how unfortunate it was that I didn't really get a handle on my weight.'"

"Oh, no," I whisper. "I'm so sorry."

When I look at her eyes, I realize that there is more to it.

"What else?" I ask.

"Nothing, it doesn't matter."

"What else happened?"

"I heard your mom mention something," she says reluctantly.

I fold my fingers into my palm and press until it hurts.

"What did she say?" I ask, clearing my throat.

"She said how pretty I would be if I were to lose all of this weight."

"I'm so, so sorry," I say, putting my arm around her shoulder.

"I don't know why I'm telling you any of this. You must think that I'm a total idiot. I mean, we were friends all those years ago, but you don't even know me."

I take a deep breath.

"Karlie," I say slowly, parsing my words. "The thing is that I don't have any friends. It's so stupid to say out loud because I have all these people around me but I don't have any *friends*. And you are the first person who has actually been honest with me about, well, anything."

"I thought that you would be mad about me saying that about your mom," Karlie admits.

"Maybe I should be. But I know that's exactly the kind of thing that she would say."

We hold each other for a few moments.

"So why did you tell me?" I ask.

"I don't know, I guess I just felt like it. Maybe I wanted to see who you really are. I mean, we are connecting and having fun, but I don't really know you. I thought you would get mad and just push me away."

"I'm glad you told me," I say quietly.

I take a sip of my wine and let it linger in my mouth for a few moments.

"This is the first honest conversation that I've had in a very long time. Ever since my breakup with... Henry."

"Henry? Who is Henry?"

"He's my ex-boyfriend. No, he's more

than that. He's a man that I thought that I was going to marry."

"But you are marrying Franklin Parks, right?"

"Yes, we are engaged."

Karlie keeps asking me more questions about Franklin and Henry, questions that I cannot answer truthfully. Given how honest she has been with me, I don't want to lie.

"How long have you been dating?" she asks.

"About a month," I say.

This is the truth on paper, but technically it's a lie. We haven't been dating at all. But I don't know her well enough to tell her this quite yet.

"A month doesn't seem like a very long time, but your mother and your friends seem to be really excited for you."

"All that Ellis cares about is the fact that I'm marrying someone so prominent."

"And what about your mother?"

I swallow hard and then take a deep breath.

"I can't tell you everything right now," I say. "There are a lot of things going on and a lot of things that are beyond my control. But I don't want to mislead you and I don't want to lie to you because I haven't talked like this with anyone in a long time and I don't wanna lose that."

"Okay," she says slowly. "I guess I can understand that."

I let out a sigh of relief, thinking that the conversation is finally over. But then she turns to me and takes my hand in hers.

"I just want you to know that you don't have to marry him. You shouldn't have to marry anyone you don't love. And it doesn't matter how much of the wedding planning is done and it doesn't matter that you have already spent $85,000 on the wedding dress."

I take a deep breath and exhale.

I wanted someone to say this out loud just to know that I'm not insane for thinking this.

But she doesn't know the details.

She doesn't know the conditions that I'm under or the fact that I don't really have a choice.

13

AURORA

Karlie and I spend the whole afternoon together and, afterward, I invite her to my apartment for dinner. She is not supposed to stay long but we end up talking and laughing well into the night.

It feels as if no time has passed. It's as if we are back to being those silly little girls without a worry in the world.

A couple of times over the evening, I'm tempted to tell her the truth, but I bite my tongue and stop myself.

It's not that I don't trust her.

It's more than that.

I don't trust myself.

I don't know what I'm getting into with this marriage and I don't know what I will have to do to get out of it. The bargain right now is that I marry him in exchange for him saving the company and my father's life, keeping him out of prison and who knows what else.

But I don't plan on staying in this marriage for long.

I've considered the fact that it may be easier to not marry him at all, but the pressure is too much right now.

There are authorities looking into my father's dealings and I need them to stop.

Franklin has made that happen for now.

I also want my father's health to improve. And then when things calm down, that's when I will make my exit.

At least, that's the plan.

I can't tell Karlie any of this because the fewer people that know the real reason that I'm marrying Franklin the better.

"I know that we haven't talked much about your upcoming wedding," Karlie says when we open a third bottle of wine. "And I'm totally going to respect the fact that you can't tell me everything about it, but why don't you tell me a little bit about Henry?"

The sound of his name makes my throat close up.

I look down at my fingers and pick at my nails.

"What do you want to know?" I ask.

"Anything you want to tell me."

"I don't know where to start."

"Who is he?" she asks.

"He's a writer," I say. "When we met, he was working on my father's boat, as crew. But he was an English teacher during the school year at an underprivileged school. Then they opened a new division at Tate Media and my father offered him a job there. He is now the host of a very popular podcast."

"Really? Which one? I love podcasts. Especially true crime ones."

"Well, you might know this one. It's called *Generation Crime with Henry Asher*."

"Oh my God! You dated Henry *Asher*?"

I shrug. "Yeah, so what?"

"Do you know how famous he is?"

"No, I guess not."

"In online true crime circles, Henry is a God."

I laugh. This makes me really happy. I've always known that Henry was really talented and was a great storyteller and I'm really glad that he found his niche.

"The thing is that his job is sort of why things fell apart between us. He was always traveling and we weren't connecting really well and then one day we sort of broke up."

"Why didn't you get back together?" Karlie asks.

"I was angry at him. He missed my graduation and we were on these different plateaus. He kept calling me and calling me and trying to make amends and I was really angry at him. And then all the stuff happened with my father and Franklin."

"What are you talking about?"

Oh, shit, I think to myself. I've said too much.

"Well, my father had a heart attack and he was arrested."

"Yes. I saw that on the news. But then they dropped the charges?"

"Yes, they did."

"Did that have anything to do with Franklin?" Karlie asks after a moment.

"Sort of," I admit.

"Well, he is pretty well-connected."

"What do you mean by that?" I ask.

"Nothing really except that his family has a lot of friends in the justice department, at least that's what all the newspaper articles insinuate."

I swallow hard.

"I'm sorry, I didn't mean to offend you," Karlie says, misreading my apprehension.

"Oh, no, it's not that. I mean, I don't really know to what extent his father has been involved with the mob or anything else, actually I've never even met him."

"Oh," she says, surprised. "And you're marrying his son?"

"Listen, I already said this but I guess I'll repeat myself. I really can't go into the details as to what is going on."

Shit, I say to myself. I should not have phrased it like that. I mean, who the hell says that about their future husband?

Karlie leaves soon after apologizing

profusely for any offense that she might've caused.

She thinks that I'm mad, but I'm not.

I'm just sorry that I can't tell her the truth.

I'm sorry that I have to keep this secret to myself when all I really want to do is tell her every last detail and to ask her to help me figure all of this out.

14

AURORA

I feel a little weird about how we leave things but decide not to call her until tomorrow.

Instead, I focus on the good.

All of this time that we have missed with each other seems to have never existed and we pick up exactly where we left off.

I wish I had told her more about Henry, but our breakup is so interconnected with my engagement to Franklin that I got off-track.

What would have I said if I could? I wonder.

Would I have told her that he was the

love of my life and I still think about him every single day?

What I have told her is that I thought that this would be just another breakup, but every day that passes the pain that I feel is somehow worse than it was the day before?

No, of course not.

I couldn't tell her any of this because then I would have no way of explaining why I'm marrying the man that I am engaged to.

I pick up my phone, keenly aware of the fact that I'm only doing this because of all the wine. Still, I can't stop my fingers from finding his name in the contacts.

He answers on the first ring.

"Aurora?" he asks groggily.

When I don't respond, he clears his throat and says my name again.

"Hi," I whisper.

It's not that I don't want to talk to him, it's that it actually hurts my heart to do so.

"Are you there?" he asks.

His voice is strong yet kind and all I wanna do is tell him how much I love him.

"Yes, I'm here," I say quietly.

Suddenly, my phone rings. I glance down and see that he's trying to FaceTime me.

My heart drops and then rises quickly up into my chest.

My hands start to shake as I press the Accept button.

"What are you doing?" I ask him. "What if Franklin was here?"

"Then you wouldn't have called me," Henry says confidently.

He holds the phone a little bit away from his face and I see the way that he tosses his hair as he talks. A few strands fall into his eyes and I can't help but lick my lips looking at his gorgeous face.

"You look beautiful," he says, staring straight into my eyes.

I give him a slight nod, fearing the fact that if I look at him long enough, I might just lose all ability to think.

"Thank you, you look pretty good yourself."

He doesn't say anything for one moment, and then another.

I don't say anything either.

Instead, we just stare like two people

who have not looked at each other in a very long time.

"I miss you," I blurt out. The words seem to just spring out of me.

His irises move from side to side as he gets closer to the phone. Peering into his eyes, I see a tear form somewhere at the bottom of his lid.

"I miss you, too," he says, biting his lower lip.

"I'm sorry, I shouldn't have said that."

"No, that's exactly what you should've said. What happened to us?" he asks. "I thought that we would be together forever. I thought that you would be the woman that I would marry."

I thought so, too, I say silently to myself. I want it to be you more than I ever wanted anything.

"Relationships are complicated," I say, clearing my throat.

I say that to let him down gently, but all I see is the pain on his face.

"When did you start seeing him?" he asks after a moment.

I take a deep breath, I don't answer. I don't know how.

"You have to tell me," he insists.

Do you want me to lie? I ask him silently.

"Why did you get engaged so quickly?" Henry demands to know.

He props his head up with his hand and peers at me.

He deserves to know the truth, but not the real truth.

But what if I told him what is really going on? Maybe he could help me?

This thought and about a hundred others similar to this one rush through me.

I want him to know the truth more than anything and yet I can't bring myself to tell him. Why?

If Henry knew then I wouldn't be able to go through with it; I wouldn't be able to marry Franklin. And I have to do it, otherwise, I lose everything.

"Tell me about your work." I try to change the subject.

"No, tell me about your fiancé," he insists.

"I don't want to talk about this."

"I don't want you to marry him."

"I know that, and I'm sorry. But that's exactly what's going to happen."

"Do you even love him?"

I am surprised by this line of questioning, with him dancing so close to the truth.

"Of course, I love him," I say, keenly aware of precisely how unconvincing I am.

"What do you love about him? Do you love the fact that he sleeps with every single woman who walks through his office? Do you love the fact that he denigrates women? Do you love the fact that there are rumors about him being into underage girls?"

His questioning draws all of the air out of my lungs. I didn't know any of this.

I mean, I've heard some of the rumors and I know that he's a womanizer, but underage girls?

No, that can't be true.

Can it?

"You don't know anything about him, Aurora," Henry insists. "He just fed you a few lines to try to make you fall in love with him. He has done the same thing to thousands of other women. They all fall for it and now you have as well."

"You don't know the first thing about me," I say sternly.

"I know that you are much better than Franklin Parks. I know that you deserve someone who will treat you like a goddess."

"Do you mean like you treated me?" I ask and all the air is sucked out of the room.

15

AURORA

Henry pauses for a moment, realizing that he has stepped into a big hole.

"No, better than I ever treated you. Listen, I know that I was an asshole. I shouldn't have missed your graduation and I shouldn't have put my work before you so much. But this is the first job that I was really excited about and I thought that I finally had a chance to write and do something meaningful."

"Yeah," I say quietly. "I understand."

"Of course it's not lost on me the fact that he's my boss. If you were to break things off, I would probably lose my job and

I wouldn't expect anything else. But I don't care. I don't care about that, not as much as I care about you."

"I never wanted you to quit your job, that's why I helped you get it in the first place. I thought it was a great opportunity and I'm glad that you are so well and you have such a great following. You're doing really good work and it shows."

I pause, trying to think of what else to say and then just close my mouth and say nothing.

"Can I ask you something?" Henry asks.

"Sure," I say, nodding.

"Do you love him?"

Not this again, I resist the urge to roll my eyes.

"Yes," I lie.

"No, you don't," he challenges me.

I shake my head and stare at him, into those piercing eyes that once belonged to me.

"I don't know what you want from me," I say after a moment. "If you don't want to believe me then don't, but it's the truth."

"You're a very good liar, Aurora, but I know that you're lying."

"Whatever," I say, waving my hand at him, pushing my anger away.

"Can I ask you something else?"

"You don't have to ask my permission to ask me things, I'm here, talking to you. Just ask me," I blurt out.

"Did you cheat on me?"

This takes me by surprise.

"No," I say quietly. "I never cheated on you and I would never do that to you. I would never do that to anyone."

"Why do I get the feeling that you're lying?" He narrows his eyes.

"Because you're full of shit," I say with anger spilling out of me.

My chest gets hot and my hands form into fists.

"Who do you think you are?" I ask him. "If you think that I cheated on you, then you don't know the first thing about me. And you're an asshole for even thinking that."

"I'm sorry, okay? I'm really sorry."

"I don't care," I say. "I loved you, more than I ever loved anyone. And you didn't give a shit! I'm glad that you got a job, a career out of this, but I thought that we would be together forever, too. I just got tired of fighting and I got tired of the distance. I wanted you to be with me and you didn't want to."

"I'm sorry that I took you for granted," Henry says.

"Now, it's too late."

"No, it's not. Don't marry him."

"You don't get to tell me what to do," I say.

"Of course not, I'm not trying to. Except that, please don't marry him. He's an asshole. He's smart and attractive, but he doesn't care about you. He doesn't care about anybody."

He's not wrong, but I can't very well admit that.

"How did he even ask you? How did you even get together?" Henry asks.

I don't know what to say. I don't know what the right story is, not really.

"I knew him from before. He helped my father out of a jam and we sort of started talking and things went from there."

"Is he a good kisser?" Henry asks.

"You don't get to ask me that," I say.

Henry clenches his jaw and then relaxes. I want to tell him more than anything that I have no idea what kind of kisser Franklin is because I've never kissed him, but I keep my mouth shut.

This is all for the greater good, I tell myself, trying desperately to believe it.

"Can we talk about something else?" I ask after moment.

I don't want to hang up yet, I want to keep talking to him but I can't stand to talk about Franklin anymore.

"Sure, what do you wanna know?"

"Tell me about your work. What are you working on now?"

"Well, actually, Franklin set me up with a really interesting story. It's about a girl who went missing in North Dakota, she went out there with her boyfriend who got a job in the oil field. The local police suspect that he did it, but there are also other suspects. I was planning on coming home, but the more that I researched the story the more I realize that it's really one that needs to be told."

"Why is that?" I ask.

"Because she was black. And unfortunately, not that many people care when black girls go missing. It's not a story that's told often and it's one I feel compelled to tell."

"So what happened to her?"

"I don't know for sure," he says. "The idea is that I would report on it as I investigate it."

"That sounds like a really interesting project," I say quietly. "I'm definitely going to listen to it."

"Do you listen to my podcast?" he asks.

"Of course," I say a little bit too quickly and then correct myself. "Yes, I've listened to a few episodes here and there."

The truth is that I have listened to every single episode of every single podcast multiple times. I listen to him when I fall asleep, just to hear the sound of his voice.

We talk for a little bit longer until the conversation runs out of steam. I want to know more about him but we only talk about his work.

At the end, I wish him well and I wish him good luck on the next story.

"By the way, Franklin invited me to your wedding."

"What?" I gasp.

"Franklin said he wasn't sure if you would invite me so he did on your behalf."

My mouth drops open as I stare at him.

"No," I say, shaking my head. "You can't come."

"Why not?"

"It wouldn't be proper."

"Says who?"

"Me, the bride."

Henry takes a deep breath and sits against the back of his chair.

"Why do you even want to come?" I ask, my whole body trembling. I'm not so sure that I will be able to go through with it with him watching.

Henry knows the truth even though he doesn't realize that he knows it. He knows it deep down, in his gut.

Henry takes a long pause. When he opens his mouth, he says, "I want to see if you will actually go through with it."

16

HENRY

I arrive at the Ritz dressed in a black tie tuxedo, which I rented earlier that day.

The rental costs me three hundred and that's way above my budget. But I can't miss seeing her in real life.

I'm supposed to be in North Dakota today, beginning my research, but I fly back just to attend Aurora's engagement party.

She told me that she didn't want to see me at the wedding, but she didn't say anything about the engagement party.

Franklin invited me to that as well, and I can't resist.

Walking through the double doors of

one of the fanciest hotels in New York City, I feel out of place. I'm pretty sure that even the doorman makes more money than I do. Still, I need to see her if only to confirm the fact that she is actually getting married.

When Aurora called me that night, I did not expect to talk to her for close to an hour. In fact, I didn't expect her to call me at all.

But she did, and now I can't stop thinking about her or the fact that she might be lying.

I used to think that she'd cheated on me, but now I'm pretty certain that she did not.

What I do think is that she's marrying him against her will.

Is that crazy?

I mean, that would never happen in this day and age.

And that would certainly not happen to an heiress, right?

I ask the doorman about the Tate/ Parks engagement party and he points me to the ballroom at the end of the hallway.

Most of the people inside are much older than I am, probably Aurora's parents' friends. There are elegant draperies all around and all the guests are dressed in gowns. The room looks like a wedding reception rather than an engagement party.

I slowly make my way toward the bar in the back and spot Franklin holding court with Aurora's father. Avoiding them, I start to make my way back around the room. When I come out of the ballroom, I run straight into her.

Without a second thought, she throws her arms around me.

"What are you doing here?" she whispers into my ear.

"I'm sorry about that," she says, pulling away and hiding her exuberance behind a facade of appropriateness. "How are you?"

"I'm good, how are you?" I ask.

"Fine," she says quietly, looking down at her feet.

Dressed in a short black dress, with thick straps and high stilettos, she doesn't really look like the woman I used to date. This person is buttoned up and so put together that she doesn't look comfortable in her own skin.

Aurora shifts her weight from one foot to

another and looks up at me with her big wide eyes. For a second, it looks like she's pleading for me to do something. What, I don't know.

"Are you okay?" I ask, putting my hand on her arm.

She jerks it away and folds her arms across her chest. "Yes, of course, I'm fine."

We stand staring at each other, neither of us saying a word.

"Aren't you going to congratulate me?" she asks.

"Yes, of course, congratulations," I say without much fanfare.

The expression on her face changes and her plastic smile disappears.

"Why are you here?" she asks. "Are you trying to make me angry?"

"No, of course not. I just needed to see you."

"Why?"

"I miss you," I say with a shrug. "I don't know what else to say. I love you."

I know that I'm probably making things very complicated, but I want her to know the truth.

"That's not fair," Aurora says after moment. "You're too late. I am engaged to someone else."

"Someone you don't love," I point out. "Someone you are marrying because… you have to."

Her eyes get big like two saucers and her mouth drops open.

"How do you…" she lets her voice trail off.

"How do I, what?" I ask her. "How do I *know?*"

"No, I misspoke," she says. I don't believe her.

"Aurora, what is going on here? Why are you doing this?"

"I love him," she says quietly.

She stares deep into my eyes and repeats herself.

"You can trust me, you know that, right?" I ask.

She doesn't respond.

"You can trust me and you can tell me anything," I insist.

"I don't have anything to tell you," she

says after a long pause. "Why can't you understand that?"

"Tell me the truth," I plead with her. "I can help you."

Her eyes dart back-and-forth and then she looks down at her hands.

I can feel that she's on the verge of telling me something. And then Mrs. Tate appears.

Aurora folds her arms across her chest and puts up an invisible wall between us.

"Mom, do you remember Henry?" Aurora asks.

"Yes, of course. It's very nice to see you again," Mrs. Tate says. "I've heard that you are having a lot of success with your podcast. Congratulations!"

"Thank you," I mumble.

"Aurora, honey." Mrs. Tate turns to her. "I'm sorry to pull you away but Franklin is getting ready to make a speech and he needs you by his side."

17

HENRY

I stand in the back and listen to Franklin say all sorts of nice and beautiful things about Aurora, all of which someone else must've written for him.

It's not until this speech that I fully realize that whatever this is, it is not a real marriage. Franklin doesn't know the first thing about her, and, for some reason, it doesn't seem to bother Aurora.

She laughs and smiles, occasionally looking down at her feet the way that she does when she feels uncomfortable. Franklin doesn't seem to notice and continues talking extravagantly about them as a couple and mostly about himself.

Unwilling to listen to anymore of the charade, I step outside and find myself at the hotel bar near the lobby. I spot Jackie at the far end, nursing a tumbler.

"What are you doing here?" I ask, eyeing his drink and wondering what's in it.

"I was visiting a girl a few blocks away and remembered that you were going to be here," he says. When he finishes his drink, he orders another.

The bartender pours him tonic water into his glass and I let out a sigh of relief.

Dressed in a leather jacket and with his black hair slicked back, Jackie Peterson looks every bit like the PI that he is.

"I can confirm that there was an investigation into William Tate's affairs and they were looking for evidence of insider trading and embezzlement. But as soon as Aurora agreed to marry Franklin Parks, all charges were dropped."

"But how could they do that?" I ask. "I mean, they already arrested him. Didn't they have to explain it to a judge?"

"What can I tell you?" Jackie asks.

"Franklin and his family are very well connected."

"His family?"

"Yes, his father knows everybody, and whoever he doesn't know Franklin knows."

"William Tate did have a heart attack. I know that you had your suspicions, but there are hospital records to substantiate that. He really had no idea that he was getting arrested. Another thing that I found out is that he has been going to almost everybody he can think of to find a buyer for Tate Media. But he wanted too much. No one would value it as high and he refused to budge."

"Why?" I ask.

"I suspect that he had taken so much money out of the company's coffers that if he were to sell it for any less, there wouldn't be much left."

"Where does Franklin come in?" I ask.

"Franklin started OMS but his family has a lot of holdings in various oil fields as well as real estate companies. His father also owns a very profitable chain of storage units, the biggest one in the country. The storage industry is one of the biggest growth sectors right now with everyone buying way too much crap and needing space to store everything in."

"What does this have to do with Aurora?" I ask.

"I'm not really sure," he says. "But somehow she is part of the deal. I heard that her father had made a proposition to Franklin before about selling part of Tate Media to him, but he was never interested. And then suddenly, a month after your breakup, her father is arrested and they announce their engagement. One of the sources that I've talked to said that she was part of the deal."

"Part of the deal?" I gasp.

"It's the only reason why William Tate is out of jail right now and moving up the rungs of the richest men in the world."

"Because she agreed to marry him?" I ask.

"Looks like it." He nods.

"But why? Why does he want to marry her?"

"*That* I do not know."

"No," I say, shaking my head. "This can't be happening. I mean, this can't be true."

"It's the only thing that would explain why this is happening so quickly. Unless of course, you actually believe that they are in love."

I want to believe that.

I want to believe that more than anything because then it would mean that she's not being forced to marry someone against her will.

"How do you know that the charges were dropped after they announced the engagement?" I ask.

"I have some connections in the justice department and the police and that's the rumor. No one will go on record, of course, but these things did not happen without some serious pull from the higher ups."

"So, what do you think?" I ask, turning toward him.

"There's definitely something here," Jackie says. "But if you want to investigate further, you have to know who you're dealing with. You have to be really careful about what you say and to whom, even Aurora.

She doesn't seem to have much of a choice in any of this and she may be playing her own game, one that may require her to sacrifice you if it came right down to it."

I shake my head and finish my whiskey.

"I know that you don't want to believe that," Jackie says, "but I want you to really think about this. He's not *just* your boss, he's one of the most powerful men on earth. What you're talking about is investigating and exposing him for whatever it is that you may find. But in doing so, he will probably take down Aurora's father as well. If she's doing this to protect him, then she will not go along with it quietly. And if you're doing this to get her back, that may not work."

"Well, hello there," Franklin says, walking up to us.

My heart drops into the pit of my stomach.

My ears start to buzz as blood rushes through my head.

What did he hear?

How much did he hear?

"Aren't you going to congratulate me?" Franklin asks.

18

HENRY

When I rise to my feet, my knees wobble but I force myself to stand up and give him a warm hug.

"Congratulations," I say. "I'm really happy for you."

I introduce him to Jackie.

"You used to be a cop, right?" Franklin asks.

"Yes, at the Montauk Police Department."

"What happened with that?"

"I had some issues with the way that the department was being run so I decided to strike out on my own."

"That's a massive understatement." I chuckle to myself.

Jackie lost his job because he threatened a fellow police officer with a gun at the station after that guy found out Jackie was sleeping with his wife. But that's not exactly the sort of thing you tell your potential new employer.

"Besides, the pay is much better as a PI."

"I like that," Franklin says. "Well, if my man here says you're the one for the job, who am I to argue with him?"

"Thanks, I appreciate that," I say.

"When are you planning on going there?"

"In a few days," I tell him. "I want to spend some time with my mom first."

We chat for a while and everything is pleasant. He's actually quite a likable guy.

"So, what sort of things do you usually investigate?" Franklin asks Jackie after ordering another drink.

"Ah, the usual things. A lot of stalking of married people to find out if their spouse is cheating so that they can use that evidence in their divorce and custody cases. Maybe, I should give you my card," Jackie jokes.

Franklin shakes his head. "Nope, that's not gonna happen to us," he insists.

"They all say that." Jackie laughs. "In that case, maybe I should give my card to Aurora. I mean, you do have quite a reputation."

Franklin stops laughing and any inkling of a smile disappears.

"Nope, not anymore," he says after a moment. "Aurora is the one."

My heart sinks into the pit of my stomach.

Is he telling the truth?

Are they really together?

I had come here thinking that she was doing all of this to help her father, but what if I'm wrong?

What if she's actually in love with him?

As I try to think of a way to extricate myself from the situation, things only get worse.

Franklin sees Aurora across the room and calls her over.

"Listen, I think I have to go," I say and start to walk away, but Franklin stops me.

When Aurora gets to his side, he puts his arm around her and gives her a big kiss on the mouth.

I want to punch him in the face, but I bury my fists in my pockets.

"Just wanted to see if you guys are planning on becoming friends anytime soon," Franklin says confidently.

Aurora and I look at each other and then down at the floor, without saying a word.

"I know that you have been through a lot but I like having both of you in my life and it would be good if you could be friends."

"Are you kidding me?" I want to ask. "Why is he doing this? Is this his idea of a joke?"

I don't know Franklin well enough to make a judgment either way, but I get the feeling that he's being genuine.

When I look up at Aurora, she shakes her head a little bit from side to side and only meets my eyes for moment.

"Listen, bro, I want to introduce you to

someone," Franklin says. "I think you're really gonna like her."

"No, no thanks." I start to protest, but it's already too late.

He waves to a beautiful woman with lustrous blonde hair and perfect sky-high breasts.

"This is my old friend, Chelsea Novak."

Despite her perfect exterior, there is something fragile about Chelsea that draws me in immediately.

When we shake hands, she gives Franklin a brief hug of congratulations. They look like they have been friends for a long time. There is no tension between them. In fact, this is the most comfortable that I have seen Franklin with a woman and I wonder if she is actually an old flame of his.

We make small talk about nothing in particular and Jackie excuses himself when the conversation runs a little dry. The thing is that it's not really a four-way conversation, it's mainly just Chelsea and Franklin catching up while Aurora and I stand around waiting for something to say without actually doing it.

I'm not sure what exactly Chelsea does, but judging from her gown and the way that she handles herself, I can tell that she has been a very wealthy woman for a long time.

When the conversation shifts to the stock market, which it inevitably does, she mentions that she had followed his advice and became an angel investor in a number of up-and-coming tech companies.

Franklin laughs and says that he's glad that his suggestions have paid off.

"Well, you know, I've never been involved with anything like that and I'm glad that you showed me the ropes."

"And now you're an expert, from what I hear."

"No, of course not. Not like you."

"Ha." He laughs. "That's not what Jimmy tells me."

"Who is Jimmy?" Aurora asks.

"He runs the entire angel investor fund that we are both heavily invested in," Franklin explains. "You see, I had to drag this girl, kicking and screaming, to make an investment and I step away from that business for a little bit and come back to discover that she is actually the one who is making the most money."

Chelsea laughs and tosses her hair, waving her finger in his face.

"Jimmy tells me that you've gotten quite involved, picking companies, suggesting companies—"

"Oh, come on," she says. "There's only so much shopping that I can stomach."

I don't really care about listening to any of this.

They are just two people who have more money than they know what to do with, trying to figure out how to get more. Yet, there's something that draws me in.

Aurora is part of this world.

I never had any interest in anything but having a comfortable life, and then I met her.

Suddenly, I realize just how complicated being rich can really be.

When Franklin and Chelsea get closer and start talking more intimately, I see my chance to pull Aurora away.

"Congratulations," I say, offering to order her another drink.

She shakes her head. "No, thank you."

"Are you having a good time?" I ask.

"Yes, of course, what would make you think that I'm not?" she asks defensively.

"I wasn't trying to imply that," I say, leaning on the bar and squaring myself off with her. "If there's something that you want to tell me, anything at all, I want you to know that you always can."

"I don't know what you're talking about," she says after a long pause, even though we both know that she does.

"Hey, listen, we're missing the whole party," Franklin says, dropping his arm around my shoulder. "Why don't we go back inside and take our girls out on the dance floor?"

19

AURORA

I watch them from afar and I can't help but feel jealous.

Why did Franklin have to introduce him to *her*, of all people!

Chelsea is tall, beautiful, flirtatious, smart, and wealthy. She has made her money in real estate and investing. But she was one of the earliest investors in Snapchat and Uber and she made out with multiple millions. Now, she even has a makeup line that is doing so well that it has landed her on the cover of Forbes.

I'm not sure if Henry knows any of this, but he is certain to find out as soon as he Googles her.

Franklin holds me in his arms and grinds against me as the lights dim and the music gets louder and all I can focus on is Henry and Chelsea and the way that his hands make their way down her body.

It occurs to me that I have never danced with Henry before and I never knew that he was such a good dancer.

But then again, he is amazing in bed so why wouldn't he be amazing on the dance floor?

When I can't stand watching them anymore, I try to pull away from Franklin, who stops me in my tracks.

"No," he says. "Let's dance some more."

"No, I don't want to," I say.

I try to walk away, but he grabs my wrist.

He clenches his jaw and tightens his grip around my wrist, pulling me closer.

"I told you that I want to keep dancing," he says.

I've never seen this side of him before. I shake my head but when a new song starts, I do as he says.

"Good," he whispers into my ear. "You look good out here."

He runs his hands up and down my body and I hate the way that it feels.

The first time that he kissed me was right there, right in front of Henry. He even stuck his tongue down my throat and it was everything I could do not to push him away and pretend it wasn't happening.

"I think it's about time that we took things to a new level, don't you?" Franklin asks.

With his hand on the small of my back, he pushes me closer to him. He lifts my chin up to his face and presses his lips onto mine.

I don't want to kiss him back so I keep my lips perfectly still.

Please, make this go away, I say to myself.

But of course, it doesn't.

I said that I would marry him.

We are engaged.

Kissing him is the least that I will be expected to do.

Why am I doing any of this again? I think to myself.

Perhaps, there's another way. Perhaps

there's some way that I can get somebody else on my side.

Maybe I should reach out to Henry, maybe I should tell him the truth.

But then in the corner of my eye, I see my mother. She stands on the sidelines, against the wall, talking to our family attorney.

My father is doing better, but he's not well. If I were to break up with Franklin, especially now, after we have announced our engagement in such a public manner and all of New York is expecting to see a lavish wedding, then he is going to make me regret everything that I have done.

I may not have a close relationship with my father, but he is still my father. I love him, but mostly I love what he has built. There are thousands of people working at Tate Media and if he were to go down, they would all lose their jobs and many of them would not recover.

No, this isn't just about me or my family.

I have to save Tate Media for something greater. And if I were to break up with him, no, *when* I break up with him, it will be on my own terms. I will walk out of this relationship, if you can call it that, with my head held high and my company securely in my possession.

I glance back at Henry and see them dancing together, with her arms firmly around him. I want to walk over there and push myself in the middle of them and let Henry take me into his arms, but instead I take a deep breath and focus my attention on my fiancé.

I look into his eyes, pull him closer to me, and this time I press my lips onto his.

I open my mouth slightly and my tongue searches for his. His kiss is soft and effervescent, much different than it was the first time.

He isn't trying to force me. Instead I am leading him along the way.

When I pull away from him and look up into his eyes, a big smile washes over his face.

"What was that?" Franklin asks. "Have you changed your mind about me?"

"I don't know about that," I say with a

smile at the corner of my lips. "But let's just say that you have my attention."

He likes that and he tries to kiss me again, but I put my finger up to his lips.

"Not quite yet," I say, fluttering my eyelashes. "Let's take this a little slow."

"No, I can't take it any slower. If you were anyone else, we would've already slept together twice, I wouldn't have called you for three days."

I laugh.

"Well, I'm not anyone else. My name is Aurora Penelope Tate and you have never met a woman like me before."

I open my mouth and lick my bottom lip. Then I bite it a little bit, as if I'm a shy girl in the corner, inexperienced in the ways of the world.

I pick up a strand of my hair and curl the end around my finger. Then I raise my hand up to his face and run my fingers along his jawline.

Standing on my tiptoes again, I bring my face so close to his that I can feel his breath on my lips.

"Kiss me," I tell him.

He does what I say and I kiss him back.

I don't want to kiss him.

I don't want to be anywhere near him, but this is the only way that I can get the upper hand in this relationship.

If I'm going through with this, then I have to be the one in power. He has to listen to me. I can't let him boss me around.

Everything that is going to happen between us sexually is going to be on my own terms.

When I pull away from him, I glance over his shoulder and see Henry's wide eyes, with a look of utter disappointment in them.

He shakes his head and walks away from us.

I want to run after him, but I force myself to stand still.

"Poor guy," Franklin says. "He is still not over you. That's why I introduced them."

"What are you talking about?" I ask.

"Well, she just broke up with her boyfriend and she's sort of on the prowl. Nothing serious but then again Henry might be just the right guy for her."

"Henry is not very good at *not* being serious," I point out.

"That's exactly what I'm talking about," Franklin says, shrugging his shoulders. "She's always dating these alpha assholes who treat her like shit. She has enough money she doesn't need to date anyone to get anything anymore. So I thought that maybe she and Henry would be a good match."

"So, now you're playing matchmaker?" I ask.

"Well, I do have a lot of skills. I've never tried matchmaking but who knows, right?"

I shake my head, not sure how to respond.

"Don't worry about it," Franklin says. "Henry's in good hands. Chelsea is not going to hurt him."

I glance down at my shoes, fighting back tears.

I can't let him know how much I still care, but I also can't force my eyes back to his face in case a rogue tear slides down my cheek.

"Chelsea is actually a very sweet girl," Franklin says. "We messed around a little bit.

I called it messing around, but she called it dating."

"You cheated on her?" I ask.

"Well, I wouldn't call it that." Franklin laughs. "I wouldn't say that we were ever really that exclusive."

"Did she think that you were exclusive?" I ask.

"Listen, I guess I should tell you this even though this is probably not the right place, but when we were together, Chelsea got pregnant. I wasn't very happy about that fact. I tried to get her to have an abortion, but she refused. She never really wanted kids but when she found out that she was pregnant suddenly she just decided that she was going to be a mother. Anyway, things didn't work out very well. She had a miscarriage and she was really torn up over the whole thing. I had a big deal to close in Switzerland and she was quite mad when I left her at the hospital."

"You left her at the hospital?" I ask. "After she lost your baby?"

"Listen, I have a very important business to run. Lots of people and families depend on what I do and what kind of deals I make."

He laughs it off, and I can't tell if he actually doesn't care or is just pretending not to.

"As you can imagine, after that our relationship was a little bit on the rocks."

"Yes, I can see why," I say.

"But I think we got past that. She started dating every twenty-year-old that she could get her hands on and, frankly, so did I."

"So, why did you introduce her to Henry?" I ask.

"Well, he's not really part of our circle. That is a good thing. I mean, I got to know him through his work and through our phone calls and I actually really like the guy, despite the fact that he fucked you. So, I thought that maybe he might just be the right guy for *her*."

I steel my eyes and look directly into his.

What is he getting at with all of this? I ask myself.

"You wouldn't be doing all of this just to make sure that Henry and I are broken up for good?" I ask, half joking.

"What are you talking about? he asks innocently.

"First, you break us up by sending him away on one business trip after another and, now, you're setting him up with an old girlfriend?"

"Does that seem suspicious to you?" Franklin asks, pulling me closer to him and grinding harder against my body as the music starts to pick up. This is the last place that I thought we would be having this conversation and yet it seems to be the most natural and appropriate one. The music is so loud that you can barely hear yourself think. Even though we are surrounded by people, we're completely alone.

"I don't know yet," I say, smiling to ease the tension. "Let's just say you might be the nicest person in the world or the most conniving."

He pushes my hair off my neck and kisses me again. His lips linger slightly on my neck and slowly make their way up to my lips.

My mouth opens and our tongues

intertwine. To get past it, I imagine that he is someone else.

I imagine that I'm kissing Henry. But then he pulls away.

"I can't wait until tonight when we can finally be together," he whispers into my ear, making my skin crawl.

20

AURORA

Despite everything that I have thought about during our engagement, for some reason I haven't given sex much consideration.

It wasn't until we were on the dance floor that I realized that I should take more initiative in order to have more control of this aspect of my life. But then when Franklin whispered those words into my ear, whatever initiative I wanted to take suddenly dissolved.

All I wanna do is run away from here. I don't want to be with him and I don't want him to touch me.

It's not that he isn't attractive, he is, it's

just that this whole arrangement makes me sick to my stomach.

Still, I said that I would marry him and there are certain expectations that come with that.

Of course, I can fight him on it, but that would just make him more suspicious of my actions. If I want him to trust me and if I want him to let his guard down, then I have to have a good time with him.

I don't see Henry much after that. He disappears somewhere with Chelsea's hand around his waist and I am only left to wonder what they are doing tonight.

He doesn't know about my arrangement and he believes that I am actually with Franklin because I love him. I know that he doesn't have those strong feelings for Chelsea, not yet, but that's not gonna stop him from going to bed with her.

We are no longer together and yet the only thing I can think of is how long it will take for me to spend the night with Franklin.

I follow Franklin up to the penthouse, fifty floors above the engagement party. He has rented the whole upper floor, and it consists of about seven bedrooms. We have it for the night, or for however long we want to be here.

"Did you have a good time?" Franklin asks.

He pours himself a nightcap of a glass of whiskey and asks if there's anything that I want. I go to the huge walk-in refrigerator and grab an orange. I pour myself a glass of water and peel the citrus very slowly.

Despite all the food and the hors d'oeuvres that have been circling the place, I haven't had much to eat and my mouth salivates.

"Are you hungry?" he asks.

"Yeah, I haven't had much to eat."

"Well, help yourself to anything in there or, if you want, I can even whip you up something.'

"You?" I ask

"Yes, I actually am quite good at cooking."

I laugh.

"You don't believe me?" he asks.

I shake my head and bite into the first slice.

"I guess I'll have to show you one of these days," he says. "I don't even have a personal chef at home. I like cooking so much."

I feel my eyebrows raising to the middle of my forehead. Not having a personal chef is practically unheard of in our circles. I didn't even know how to make an omelet until I went to college.

"I guess there's a lot I don't know about you," I admit.

"Actually, you don't know the first thing about me. And I don't know the first thing about you. I thought that maybe we could talk a little bit and learn a few things."

I wrap my orange in a paper towel and bring it over to the oversized mid-century modern couch, overlooking the New York skyline.

I sit down and curl my feet up underneath my butt and invite him to take the seat next to me.

"What else don't I know about you?" I ask.

"There was a girl I loved once," he says without missing a beat. "I was fifteen years old, she was sixteen, and she was my first love. We talked about getting married, if you can believe that. We were stupid little kids and yet she was the only thing that made any sense to me."

I lean against the back of the couch and wait for him to continue. I've never seen this side of him before. I don't think many people have.

"To cut a long story short, she died," he says, looking down at his hands and rubbing his thumb against his index finger.

"She died?" I gasp. "How?"

"In a car accident. It was completely out of the blue. Killed by a drunk driver. There was a trial and he got ten years in prison. This wasn't the first time that he was driving drunk and this wasn't the first time that he had actually hit someone.

"The whole thing was a big fluke but it changed the course of my life. I don't know where I would be if she were still around. I know for sure that I'd be a different person. Kinder. Nicer."

I don't know what to say. Instead, I walk over to him and take his hands into mine.

"Thank you for telling me," I say. "I had no idea that anything like that happened to you."

"I know," he says. "No one does. I mean, my parents knew her. But the extent to which I loved her and the extent to which we had planned to spend our lives together, no one knows except for you."

"Why are you telling me this?"

"I don't know," Franklin says, shaking his head.

He shrugs and tries to get up but I keep holding onto his hands and pull him back down.

"Don't," I say. "Stay with me."

This is the first time that it feels like we have made a connection since I met him and I don't want it to sever.

Maybe he doesn't have to be a mystery. Maybe I just didn't bother to get to know him earlier.

"Why are you telling me this?" I ask again.

He looks up into my eyes and holds his gaze there for a little bit.

"I guess I trust you," he says after a

moment. "I guess I want you to know something about me that's real. You know what I mean?"

I nod and lean closer to him.

He runs his fingers down my neck and draws me closer to him. I put my head on his shoulder. There's still so much left unsaid between us and yet there's a tenderness that is forming that is difficult to explain.

I expect him to kiss me again and lead me toward his bedroom, but he doesn't.

He simply waits for me to kiss him. I do. Slightly, only a little bit, and then pull away.

"I'm not gonna make you do anything you don't want to do, Aurora," he says.

"I nod, I appreciate that," I say.

"But I do hope that we can be together sometime soon."

"Me, too," I say.

Again, I wait for him to make a move, and again he doesn't.

He's either very good at playing games or he is being genuine. I don't know him well enough to judge the difference but I intend to find out.

We sit together for a while without

saying a word. I wonder who this man is that I have agreed to marry, but I'm starting to realize that I don't know the first thing about him.

I had written him off as a womanizer and an asshole, but maybe I was wrong.

Maybe there is more to him than meets the eye.

Maybe we can actually find common ground.

Maybe we can make this work.

Franklin looks over at me and gives me a small smile. I smile back. Then he leans over and puts his hands in between my knees.

He pushes me against the back of the couch and kisses me hard.

So hard that it almost hurts.

"What are you doing?" I manage to get out. "Let me go!"

"Come on, Aurora, tell me that you don't want this."

"I don't want this."

He kisses me harder. He pushes me onto the couch and climbs on top of me.

My head is spinning.

What is happening right now?

I thought that we had made this connection and now this?

I have to make him stop. But how?

I try to push back but I can't budge him. I'm tempted to bite him, but I'm afraid of making things worse.

With his hands running up and down my sides, he's already doing things that I don't want him to do.

What would happen if I actually made him mad?

I freeze and lie there quietly for a few moments, hoping that he will stop.

But he doesn't. He just takes it as a sign that I'm interested.

"Stop, please stop," I whisper into his ear and push against him again.

"Come on, please don't be like that," he pleads and grabs at my breasts. "Just relax, you're going to have fun, I promise. Everyone does."

I really doubt that, I think to myself but don't dare say it out loud.

And then, something occurs to me. I don't know if this will be a turn-off or maybe even a turn-on, but it's the only thing that I can possibly say to get him to leave me alone. What if it doesn't work?

"Actually, I'm on my period," I say quietly.

He pauses. He lifts himself up off of me and stares into my eyes.

I shrug and look down, as if I am apologizing.

"Oh, shit, why didn't you say something earlier?"

"It's kind of a personal thing to just come out and say," I admit.

"Oh, is that why you weren't into doing it?" he asks.

I shrug and give him a slight nod. What else is there to do?

"Okay, well, let me know when that stops and we can give it another go," he says, sitting back up and straightening his suit. "You do know that we have to do this, right? I mean, we've been engaged for how long exactly?"

As he walks away from me completely unfazed, I let out a cautious sigh of relief.

I got him off of me for now, but will I be able to do it next time?

21

HENRY

The next morning I take my mom out to lunch. I haven't spent any quality time with her for a long time, though we do usually talk on the phone every other day or so.

For the last couple weeks she hasn't wanted to FaceTime, and I haven't insisted on it, and now I realize why.

I'm not sure what's wrong but somehow, she looks much older than she did before I left. It was only a few weeks ago, but she looks worn out.

She often sounded tired on the phone, but whenever I brought it up, she just blew me off.

Right now, it's nice to sit by the water and look out at the vast Atlantic Ocean. Our food arrives and I bite into my fish taco immediately. She takes her time, saying that she's not as hungry as she thought she was. She asks me to tell her about my work.

Mom has been a devoted podcast listener ever since my first episode, and she rarely has a negative thing to say about it. I appreciate that.

She was never the type to point out my mistakes and errors, and that made me a more confident person.

With the podcast, as with everything else, there are enough people in the world to criticize your work, you don't need that to also come from your family.

But today, I'm really interested in what she has to say. I tell her about the last story, and what it was like to interview the mother of the missing girl. She puts her hand over her mouth and tilts slightly to one side.

"What's wrong?" I ask.

"I'm just really sad," she says. "I mean, I know that you were doing important work but it just makes me worry about you being surrounded by all this negativity all the time."

"Don't worry about me, it's not as hard as it seems."

"See, you're already growing callous to it."

"I sort of have to. I mean, that's how it is when you're a reporter. You have to go out there and tell the hard stories. And with true crime, my focus is always on death. I don't have a chance to do those light-hearted stories where everything works out in the end. Even if there is justice, someone is dead."

"I just worry about you," my mom says, pushing her hair slightly out of her face.

"Why? I'm finally doing what I really love, storytelling. Honestly, I had no idea that this would be the direction that I would go in but now it makes perfect sense. There's so much creativity in putting these nonfiction stories to life and making people really care about them, especially care about crimes that happened a long time ago, or to underrepresented populations."

"Are you talking about your case in North Dakota?" Mom asks.

"Yeah, I am. That girl… People just forgot about her. She went missing and then her body was found and the world just kept spinning. I know that that happens all the time. There are thousands of unsolved murders all over the United States, let alone the world. But I'm in a position to do something about this one. I'm in a position to make my listeners care about her and really get involved. That's how these things get solved, long after the police forget about them."

"I understand, of course I do," Mom says, moving her food around her plate, but not taking more than a few bites.

I guess she's not hungry at all, though I didn't see her eat breakfast either or much for dinner last night.

"You know me, I love all of those true crime stories on Dateline and Oxygen. I mean, that's pretty much all I watch when I'm not watching Law and Order: SVU."

I chuckle to myself. My mom has been

watching Law and Order: Special Victims Unit for years. I have no idea how long it has been on but I think it's nearing its twentieth birthday and she has been a devout fan since I was a kid.

"I know that you're writing a lot for the show and you're doing a lot of good creative work, but what about your fiction? Are you thinking of getting back to that again?"

"Actually, yes. It's funny that you would bring it up but I have been toying with a novel that is sort of inspired by my work here. Perhaps, a psychological thriller with a dash of romance."

"Oh, that would be marvelous!" She laughs.

Mom takes a sip of her soda and then suddenly starts to cough uncontrollably. It sounds as if she's choking, so I quickly rush around the table and smack her back to try to clear her throat.

But after a few moments, I realize that she's not choking, she's actually coughing up blood.

After a few more violent outbursts, my

mom slides off the chair and falls down to the floor.

"Mom! Mom!" I yell for her to come back to me. "Somebody help me! Please call an ambulance!"

.

22

HENRY

Everything moves in slow motion in the waiting room except for the beating of my heart. The walls are painted a soothing pink color that is neither soothing nor particularly pink.

The chairs are plush and worn out, but not to the point of any physical deterioration like holes. But when you sit on them, you notice that they've been sat on a million times before.

I pick at the little indentation in the armrest that someone has left with a pen. Someone else had made it bigger and deeper with a different color ink. I rub my finger into it again and again but it doesn't make the anxiety go away.

The doctor comes out through the double doors with a blank expression on her face. She has done this many times before.

There is no one else in the waiting room, but she still takes me through the double doors where we can have some privacy.

This isn't good. I've interviewed enough people with their interactions with the police and medical personnel to know that when they do this, whatever news you hear is somewhere on the spectrum from bad to terrible.

"Your mother has cancer," the doctor says and my head starts to spin. She keeps talking but I don't hear the specific words that are coming out of her mouth. She's right in front of me and yet she seems to be miles away, almost on the TV screen.

"Excuse me, can you please tell me this again?" I ask her.

Apparently, this happens all the time. She's completely unfazed and repeats what she has just said again.

All I hear are tidbits of sentences.

Cancer.

Treatable.

Serious.

Radiation.

"Do you understand what I'm saying?"
Dr. Purcella asks.

I nod even though it's a lie.

"Her condition is treatable and we are
hopeful, but we have to act aggressively if
we want to stop it from growing."

"How long have you known about this?"
I ask.

"Unfortunately, for a few weeks. We
should be a lot further along than we already
are, but the treatment is expensive and she
did not want to leave her estate with debt."

"Her estate? What estate?"

"That's just how you refer to anyone's
home ownership or anything else that they
own when you talk about their passing," Dr.
Purcella says.

I shake my head.

No, no, no. I know that, of course, I
know that.

"What does that have to do with
anything? Is she dying?"

"No, actually she's not. But only if we take aggressive action right now."

"And she doesn't want to do that?" I ask.

"No, she is being quite hesitant. The treatment is expensive and somewhat experimental, and her insurance doesn't cover it."

"Fucking money," I mutter to myself. "Why does everything in this world have to come down to that?"

"We have some money," I say. "I mean, I do. Plus she has the house."

"Listen, I can't talk to you about the financial situation, I am her doctor."

"You have to tell me the truth. What would you do if you were in my situation?"

"I would get her that treatment as soon as possible, no matter what."

"And she doesn't wanna do it because it costs too much?" I ask.

"She doesn't want to lose the house," Dr. Purcella says. "I don't know what's going to happen, but I can make you one promise. If you don't make her go through with this treatment, she is going to die. I tried to explain this to her already. I tried to tell her that her life is more important than a house, but she doesn't seem to understand that."

"I wish I'd known about this earlier," I say.

Dr. Purcella shrugs.

"I wish I could have reached out to you, but I'm her doctor and our conversations are privileged. However, now that she is unconscious and you are her next of kin, I am telling you this because I hope that you can help me save her life."

After Dr. Purcella leaves, I wander around the waiting room for a long time.

It looks as if I'm trying to decide something but in reality, I'm just trying to figure out a way to convince my mother to let me help her.

I realize the risks with the treatment.

Nothing is guaranteed.

But when I look up Dr. Purcella online and research the treatment that she recommended I have hope.

Unfortunately, it is very expensive and experimental. Insurance companies don't want to cover it because there are no guarantees.

But there's no guarantees with radiation and chemotherapy either.

Apparently, my mother has known about this for weeks and did not bother to tell me. We have talked on the phone many times and still she kept this from me.

Now, I realize why she looked so tired and worn out when I finally saw her in person after all this time. The cancer is eating away at her and she's doing nothing to help herself.

A few hours later, the nurses tell me that I can go in and talk to her. I'm supposed to stay calm and not excite her but all I wanna do is wrap my hands around her shoulders and shake her as hard as I can.

"How are you doing?" I ask, walking into her room cautiously.

She opens her eyes a little bit, looks at me, and closes them again. I just sit down next to her and place her hand in mine. The room smells like antiseptic.

Everything is clean and sterile, which is a good thing, but it's also lacking humanity. My mother is attached to machines that are helping her breathe and taking away her pain, and I just hope that science is enough to keep her with me for years to come.

I sit with her for a few hours until she finally comes back to me. Her skin is sallow and her eyes look vacant.

Her mouth is dry and her lips are chapped. I bring her a cup of water, and she sits up a little to take it in.

I want to ask her how she's feeling, but I am afraid of the answer.

"I'm sorry I didn't tell you," she says, shaking her head. "I'm so embarrassed."

These words are difficult for her to say so I tap her hand to tell her to stop, but she keeps going.

"It's fine," I say quietly. Of course, it's not but now is not the right time to talk about it. "You need to get treatment."

"No, I can't. I'm going to lose the house. It's too expensive."

"I don't care, it's just money."

"Money is everything," she says.

"No," I say sternly, looking straight into her eyes. "Money is a way to get something. I'm not going to lose you over something as stupid as a house."

She starts to say something else, but I press my finger to her lips and stop her.

"I know that you have worked really hard for that house and it means everything to you. But to me, it's nothing but a house. I'd rather have my mother in my life than that piece of property."

"And what will happen after we lose the house?" she asks.

23

HENRY

I don't know what my mom is talking about and stare, waiting for her to explain.

"What are you talking about?" I ask.

"I only have the house," she says quietly. "I don't have anything beyond that. If I start this treatment, then I won't be able to work. I won't have an income coming in. What's going to happen then?"

"I don't want you to worry about any of that," I say, squeezing her hand. "You have taken care of enough, now it's my turn."

"But you can't afford it," she says, shaking her head.

I swallow hard.

She's right. I don't make very much money. I mean, I make enough for me plus some, but not enough to cover all of these medical treatments.

Besides, once she starts going to all these appointments, she will also need extra help at home. What does that mean for my job in North Dakota?

She knows all of this and that's exactly why she never told me what was happening.

"I'm really angry with you," I say after a moment.

Her eyes open wide.

"You had no right to do what you did," I say. "You should have gotten treatment when you were first diagnosed, when the doctor first told you what you needed to do. But you waited and now… What if we don't have enough time?"

"What will happen will happen," she says with a shrug.

Sometimes her defeatist attitude has been useful, especially in times when we were facing a situation that we couldn't get out of. But this isn't one of those situations.

No, this is about seizing your opportunities, and going after it with everything you have.

"I don't want you to worry about anything except for how to get better," I tell her. "You have to focus all your energy on that. Money doesn't matter. I can figure something out."

She shakes her head.

"You don't believe me?" I ask.

"I know that you have a lot of rich friends now, but that doesn't mean that you have any money."

"I know," I say quietly. "Don't you think I know that?"

"I don't know what to think," she says, turning her face away from me.

"Aurora is marrying someone else, you know that, right?"

I pull away from Mom. This is the first time that she has mentioned Aurora's name since our breakup.

"What do you want me to do about it?" I ask.

"You love her," my mother says. "Why don't you tell her?"

"Because she's engaged to someone else, and she tells me that she loves him."

"That's not good enough," she says.

I take a deep breath and exhale slowly.

"Why don't you make an agreement with me?" I ask.

"What kind of agreement?"

"You promise to begin treatment and fight this thing with every last breath in your body and, if you do, then I promise to tell Aurora how I feel about her, no matter what it costs me."

"I promise," my mom says and closes her eyes.

ON THE RIDE BACK HOME, later that evening, my mother continues to dwell about the cost of the ambulance.

"I know that it's going to be in the thousands," she says over and over.

"It is what it is. I didn't know what was going on with you. You coughed up a lot of blood and you just passed out. What was I supposed to do?"

"You were supposed to help me into the car and drive me over there," Mom says. "These things happen. But they don't have to cost $3000 for nothing."

"It's not for nothing, I already went over this," I repeat myself.

We go in circles over and over again all the way home.

She's angry at me for not saving money, and I'm angry at her for keeping her disease from me.

Despite the argument, I get the sense that we are both angry about the same thing. She's young and none of this should be happening. Still, given how much she's fighting me on this, it gives me hope that she can actually beat this thing after all.

When I get her back to her house, I help Mom to bed.

I make myself a cup of tea and sit on the same aging couch that I have sat on for years. I try to bury my worries in work. I go through my emails, but I'm too tired to write anyone back.

I open the research articles that Liam has sent me but I am too tired to read them.

The words are all jumbled and I forget what I have read in the paragraph above when I start reading the one below.

No, I'm too spent to focus. I open Netflix and lose myself in an old episode of Frasier.

It's an old 90s sitcom that I never watched when it was really on but got really into afterward.

One episode turns to into another, and another, and I start to feel a little better. Not good enough to laugh, but maybe crack a smile.

A few hours later, tired and a little bit brain dead, I finally manage to fall asleep.

THE FOLLOWING MORNING, I get up early and make my mom breakfast. There's so much that I want to talk to her about but unfortunately, I can't.

After her eggs are done, I take them to her room. But she is too tired to eat them. She opens her eyes briefly but then asks for me to leave her alone.

I end up eating her breakfast alone,

sitting at the dining room table and staring at the pile of bills that I have collected on the nearby dresser.

I'm not sure how I could have missed them before. Usually my mother keeps a very tidy house, but recently it has been nothing but a mess.

I find all of her bills in a pile right underneath a framed picture of me from ninth grade. I stare at the boy with braces and pimples and hair that's a little bit too short and a face that's a little bit too chubby and I remember how much I wanted to be a grown-up back then, and how now I wish I could just go back to being a kid again.

I take a deep breath and start going through her bills. Though she hasn't been going through the experimental treatment, she has been incurring a lot of bills for her medications.

By a lot, I mean, in the thousands. I look up the amount of the ambulance bill on my phone.

It's almost four grand. At the bottom of the stack, I find the foreclosure notices.

She has missed the mortgage payment

for the last three months, and those are just the payments that I find.

I make myself another cup of coffee as I try to figure out what to do. I finally have a steady job with prospects for the future, but my salary is nowhere near the amount that I would need to cover these payments.

Moreover, it's clear to me now that my mother will need a lot more help than I had realized.

I need to go to North Dakota because I need to do the story, grow my podcast, and hopefully my salary, but I also need to stay here and take care of her.

I can't afford a full-time nurse. She probably makes as much as I do a month.

What the fuck do I do?

I take a deep breath and force myself not to dwell on it for too long.

I need to reach out to Franklin.

I pick up my phone and click on his name.

After a few rings, Aurora answers.

"Shit," I say into the phone, without realizing it.

"Henry?" she asks.

I sigh loudly and shake my head. The only reason why she would be answering his phone is because she spent the night with him. I feel so stupid.

Of course, she had spent the night with him, they are engaged to be married.

She is his fucking fiancée.

"Franklin is sleeping right now," Aurora says.

"Okay, whatever, just let him know that I called," I mumble.

"I'm sorry that I answered his phone," she says quietly. "I thought it was mine."

"No, of course, it doesn't matter."

I can hear that she's about to say something else, but I hang up.

I can't stand to listen to this much longer. I want her back in my life more than I could ever explain or say and now I'm certain that it's never going to happen.

Franklin calls me back later that afternoon.

I get right to the point.

"I can't take that job in North Dakota," I say that as firmly as possible.

"Why not?"

I'm tempted to lie because I don't want to talk about this out loud, but he won't go for it unless I tell him the truth.

"My mom is really sick," I say, keenly aware of the fact that my voice cracks in the middle of the sentence. I had no idea. "She was keeping it all from me but she has cancer."

My head starts to pound as I tell him all of the details. He asks questions and listens carefully and then agrees to let me work from home.

"What are you doing tomorrow night?" Franklin asks.

"I don't know, I was supposed to be on the afternoon flight out to Fargo."

"Well, good, you're free then."

"Yes, I guess," I say.

"I'm hosting a dinner party and I'd like for you to come."

"No, I don't think-"

"Please come," Franklin says.

The tone of his voice makes it sound like it's not something that I can say no to.

Not wanting to seem ungrateful for him

being so understanding of my predicament,
I reluctantly agree.

24

HENRY

I get to Franklin's building right around 6 o'clock. It's a brand new glass development with luxurious, oversized condos. The lower end ones are around 2000 ft., which may not seem like much but is quite enormous in New York City.

There's a doorman who welcomes me in and a man who shows me to the elevator and then pushes the button. We ride up to Franklin's penthouse together.

The whole trip up, I debate as to whether or not I should tip him and realize that I don't have any cash. To say that I feel like a fish out of water would be a grave understatement. I try to make up for it with some polite conversation.

A quiet beep indicates that we have arrived on the top floor. The elevator doors open right into his apartment.

"Hey," Franklin says, walking over to me in his three-thousand dollar, perfectly tailored suit. "I'm glad you made it."

I give him a nod and we shake hands.

"How are you doing?" he asks. "How is your mom?"

Aurora and Chelsea walk out of the dining room to greet me, holding sparkling glasses of champagne and laughing.

Aurora looks breathtaking in an elegant short black dress and small heels and Chelsea is beautiful in a bright red gown with lips to match.

They're supposed to match but they don't.

"I'm sorry, I am way underdressed," I say, glancing down at my TJ Maxx sport coat that's a different shade of black from my slacks.

"You look great," Franklin says quickly.

"Come on in and let me get you something to drink."

Aurora looks me up and down and gives me a small smile.

"Don't worry about it," she whispers under her breath.

I'm not really worried, I just feel out of place.

"Is anyone else coming?" I ask when Franklin takes me to a backroom that's entirely devoted to wine and pours me a glass.

"There was supposed to be another couple but they cancelled."

The wine cellar is bigger than my bedroom at home and hosts thousands of bottles. The temperature is cooler than in the rest of the apartment and the walls make it feel like it's a cellar deep underground, somewhere in the south of France.

FRANKLIN POINTS to the bottles on the far right, in a special case and tells me that those once belonged to Thomas Jefferson.

"Planning on drinking that?" I ask.

"No, of course not," he says. "To be honest, they are probably vinegar by now. It has been that long. But you know what they say about wine connoisseurs, we are the biggest snobs. So, just the fact that it once belonged to him is enough for me to keep it up there, propped up on display."

Back in the opulent living room, Aurora comes out with the hors d'oeuvres.

"These look really good," Franklin says, and gives Aurora a peck on the cheek.

"Did you make these?" I ask her.

She gives me a slight nod.

"I'm shocked," I say. "I didn't realize you knew how to cook."

"Well, I don't," she says shyly. "But Franklin insisted on it."

"What are you doing to her?" Chelsea asks, laughing.

"Well, she's going to be my wife and I'd like to have a wife who knows how to cook."

"Then you should have married someone who already does," Chelsea says. "Are you seriously making her cook this?"

He laughs and so does Aurora, but by

the expression on her face I'm not so sure
that this is a funny matter.

What is happening here? I wonder.

Aurora has never cooked anything in her
life, beyond a few simple dishes. Besides,
everyone here except for me has had
personal chefs their whole adult lives, so why
the change now?

"You see, I'm just trying to teach Aurora
a few things. She has been pampered a little
bit too much by her parents and now that
she's going to be my wife, I'd like for her to
know where she stands."

Shivers run down my spine.

I have heard rumors about Franklin, but
this is the first time that I have ever seen this
side of him.

I glance over at Aurora and try to figure
out how she feels about this. But she just
cowers away from me.

Chelsea and I exchange a look and then
Franklin starts to laugh.

He pretends that he has been joking all
along, and after giving Aurora a slight pat on
the butt, he sends her back into the kitchen.

After we finish the plate of roasted

Brussels sprouts, Aurora brings out dinner and sets it out herself. All of the servants have been sent home and it's up to her to act as a hostess. Chelsea and I both try to help, but Franklin stops us.

"Listen, you two are guests here, she's the hostess. I want to see her set the table and show all of us a good time. I mean, come on, she's my fiancée after all. Isn't that what women do?"

"No, it's not," Chelsea says. "And you know it."

"Here, let me help you," I say to Aurora when she comes out with the main dishes.

"Sit down," Franklin tells me.

I whip my head back at him and glare into his eyes.

"Sit down," he repeats himself.

"No," I say sternly. "Your fiancée needs help and I'm going to help her."

I take the dishes away from her and place them carefully on the table.

Then I follow her back into the kitchen and carry out the utensils to set the rest of the table. While we are in there, I ask her what is going on but she just shakes her head and waves her hand at me.

"You have to tell me," I insist.

"No, I don't," she says.

"Aurora —" I grab her arm.

"Let her go," Franklin says.

I turn around and see him in the doorway staring at me.

"I was just trying…" My voice trails off.

"I know what you were trying to do. You're trying to intimidate her and I won't have it."

"No, I wasn't," I say quickly. "I was just trying to figure out what's going on here."

"Nothing is going on here. We had a bet about whether or not she can make dinner and she lost. So, here she is, making dinner."

I shake my head, not wanting to believe him. I glance over at Aurora.

"Is that true?" I ask.

"Is that true?" I ask again.

"Yes, of course it is," she says, snapping her eyes onto mine.

The four of us have dinner. At first, it's a little awkward, but Chelsea quickly takes over and makes everyone feel a lot more comfortable.

The conversation shifts from one topic to another, effortlessly and whenever I quiet down, someone else picks it up.

I don't know much about Chelsea, but I would be lying if I didn't say that I wasn't a little bit interested.

We had a good time dancing at the party and she is quite the flirt. I'm glad that the other couple canceled so that I can get to know her more.

When I ask her about her work, she

glosses over her real estate and investments and instead focuses on her charity work.

"This is what I'm really interested in," Chelsea says. "My foundation supports aims to make medical care free for sick children and we also donate to many animal rescue foundations."

When I reach for a second helping of Aurora's delicious glazed salmon, Franklin asks me about my mother.

I had not planned on bringing it up, but I don't really have much of a choice.

I tell him about the diagnosis and I reiterate how grateful I am that I can do my work from New York.

"I'm sorry again that I can't investigate that story," I tell Franklin.

"Don't worry. Of course, you need to be here. I totally understand."

As I talk about my mother, I glance over at Aurora and see her fighting back tears.

"I'm sorry, I shouldn't get so emotional," she says, wiping away a tear. "I just had no idea that you were going through this."

"I guess I should have told you earlier," I say quietly.

"How are you paying for this?" Chelsea asks after a long pause.

Under the table, I press my hands into my knees and try to contain my emotions.

"I'm taking care of it," I say quickly.

"But it must cost you a fortune," Aurora says.

"Yes, it will," I admit.

I debate as to whether or not I should go into the details of everything that I'm going through. How could these three people possibly understand?

But when I look into their faces, I see that they are open to listening.

So, why not tell them? They know that I'm not wealthy. Hell, I'm not even rich. I'm pretty sure everyone who they have in their employ make more than me, so what do I have to hide?

I take a deep breath and a big sip of my wine. Sitting back against the chair, I hold my glass out and ask, "What do you want to know?"

"Everything," Aurora says. "How much is all of this going to cost?"

"A lot," I say.

"Can you be any more specific than that?" Franklin asks.

"The ambulance bill is $3700," I say. "I'm not sure how much the emergency room bill will cost. She's behind on her mortgage payments and even got a foreclosure notice from the bank. The mortgage is just over $2000 a month. She's not even doing the experimental treatment yet and her pain medication is costing close to two grand a month. That's why she's three months behind on her mortgage."

They don't say anything so I continue.

"My mom didn't tell me any of this until she passed out at the restaurant. Actually, she was hiding it from me. She didn't want me to worry. But now things have gotten a little out of hand. I have some money saved up, but not a lot. Of course, I will save some money by moving in with her, but the treatment will probably be close to $50,000, I don't know for sure. As you, Franklin, and probably you, Aurora, know my salary is $48,000 a year."

Aurora shakes her head and bites her lower lip.

Franklin and Chelsea exchange a look that I don't quite understand.

"I know that this seems like a petty problem to you three, but it's a big deal. Please understand, I'm not asking you for anything. This is just something that I'm going through that lots of Americans are going through."

Franklin tries to say something to make me feel better, but I cut him off.

I don't need his sympathy and I don't need his pity. He asked me what I was going through and I told him.

Now, I don't wanna talk about it anymore. Luckily, Chelsea gets the point and shifts the conversation to something else.

When Chelsea helps Aurora with the dishes, Franklin pulls me aside and asks me to come with him.

Modern and white, the office is empty except for the huge glass table in the center with two enormous computer screens facing a plush swivel chair.

There are floor-to-ceiling windows on all sides, looking out onto Manhattan below.

"Wow," I say. "I have to tell you I was

expecting a dark walnut interior with bookcases and the works."

"I have a library, but it's in another part of the house. Besides I don't like it when it's dark inside and, with the weather like we have here, I wanted it to be as bright as possible."

"It's beautiful," I say.

"Listen, the reason I wanted to bring you in here is to give you something."

I give him a nod.

He takes out his phone and presses a few buttons.

"What did you want to give me?" I ask.

My phone dings.

"Why don't you open that?" he suggests.

I glance down and see that I have a notification from my banking app.

I click on the notification and my jaw drops open.

26

HENRY

I stare at my phone, unable to believe my eyes. Shaking my head, I look up at him.

"No, I can't accept this."

"You have to. I'm your boss, remember?" he says, tossing his head back with a laugh.

"Seriously, I know that you have a lot of bills and I know that you're going to have a lot of bills in the future. You're my friend and I want you to accept this money... as a gift."

"Absolutely not," I say. "If, and that's a big if, I do accept it, it will be a loan."

Franklin laughs again.

"What's so funny?" I ask.

"I know that this is a lot of money to you, but seriously this is what I make in a couple hours with my investments. It's really not a big deal and I want you to stop worrying about something so… *Insignificant*."

"It's $30,000," I say, looking up at him.

"Exactly," he says. "It's only thirty grand. I've spent more than that on wine in a month. Just take the money, it's a gift, and don't worry about it."

I shake my head, staring at my phone.

"What I do want you to worry about is the next story that you're gonna break. You're one of the best investigative journalists that I have working for me and your podcast is doing amazing on the charts, but I want it to be number one every week. That's what I want you to worry about, besides just spending time with your mom."

I don't know what to say. I thank him over and over again but words don't seem to be enough.

"If you ever need any more money for medical bills, or a nurse, or whatever, just let me know. It's really not a big deal at all."

I give him a warm hug and say, "Thank you very much. You will never know how much this means to me."

I WALK Chelsea out after dinner. She drapes her coat over her shoulders but doesn't put it on and I look at the elongated part of her neck and how beautiful it looks in the twilight.

"I'm sure that that was pretty awkward for you," Chelsea says, "given that she is your ex-girlfriend and all."

"Yeah, you would think so but it wasn't really. I'm getting used to the fact that we're not together anymore."

"Would you mind doing me a favor?" Chelsea asks.

"Sure, anything."

"Would you take me home?"

"Oh, yes of course."

"It's not because I had too much to drink," she adds. "It's just that it has been a really long time since a guy took me home and I sort of miss it."

"Really? But I heard from Franklin that you were actually dating a lot."

"That's what I want Franklin to think, but that's actually not true."

"Do tell," I say, calling an Uber on my phone.

"Well, Franklin and I have kind of a complicated relationship so I don't exactly want to tell him the truth about how little I'm dating nowadays. Especially now that he's so in love and engaged to Aurora."

On the drive over, we talk a lot about our old relationships and find out we actually have a number of things in common.

She seems to be just as heartbroken over Franklin as I am over Aurora and she even makes a joke that we should band together and try to break them up.

We talk about how we could possibly do that but neither of us come up with a feasible plan.

When I show her up to her apartment, I walk her to her door. We've both had a little bit too much to drink and one of the neighbors pokes her head out and even shushes us as if we are children.

Laughing, I follow her into her apartment.

"I have the worst neighbors," Chelsea says. "That's one of the problems of being as rich as I am and being able to afford to live where I live. I'm completely surrounded by old widows or creepy old men that feel like they can treat me like shit just because that's what they've always done to women since the fifties."

I laugh. When she misses a step and trips, I put my hand around her waist and prop her up.

Our eyes meet and neither of us look away.

She's beautiful and funny and before I know what I'm doing I feel myself pulling closer to her. With our lips almost touching, she steps up on her tiptoes and kisses me.

Her lips are soft but her mouth is strong. She buries her hands in my hair and I wrap my arms around her waist. I keep my eyes shut. When I open them for a moment, it only occurs to me that she is not Aurora.

I let out a sigh. Before I can step away, she grabs up my shirt and pulls me closer. A few moments later, we are on the kitchen floor.

"I know what you're thinking," Chelsea says.

"What?" I mumble through the kiss.

"You want me to be her."

"No, of course not."

"Yes, you do. And I want you to be Franklin."

She must be really drunk or maybe I am, but I don't know how to respond to this.

"Listen, let's just do this," she says. "I want to feel anything but pain. I want to feel something real."

I shake my head. I might have been able to do it before but now it just feels too…
Awkward.

I push away from Chelsea and get up. I walk over to the living room. I take a seat on her plush couch and stare at the unusual statue of a dragon in the corner of the room. It's nearly six-feet tall and would be overwhelming the space if there were anything else around it.

"You don't like it, do you?" Chelsea asks, plopping down on the seat next to me.

"No, not really."

"You know, you're the first person who has said that to me in a very long time." She laughs. "No, actually! I think you're the first person who has ever said anything like that to me."

"Okay, thank you, I guess," I say.

"No, thank *you*. In my life, I have a lot of yes-men and not too many people telling me the truth about, well, anything."

Chelsea gets up and walks over to the bar at the far end of the room. She pours herself a glass of wine and then asks me if I want anything.

I shake my head no. This evening has been long and drunk enough already.

"I thought that Franklin would tell you the truth," I say. "He seems like the type."

She shrugs her shoulders and sits down next to me on the couch, this time much closer.

"You would think so, but he had other problems."

I want to ask her more about him and their relationship, but something holds me back.

"Listen, it has been a long day and I have to get back home."

"To Montauk?"

"Yep," I say.

"But that's like a three-hour drive."

"That's where my mom lives."

"I'm really sorry about what she has going on," she says, pausing slightly in the middle as if saying the word cancer is just too difficult for her.

"Thank you, I really have hope that everything will be fine."

"You were so brave to just come out and tell us all about her situation."

"Yeah, I guess. Or maybe I'm just a realist. I don't know. I mean, I'm not gonna sit around a table and pretend that my life is anything like yours, so I figured why not just tell you the truth? Especially since you asked."

Chelsea moves closer to me, pressing her lips onto mine. I try to pull away, but I don't. It feels good to kiss her and I haven't felt good in a long time.

Chelsea buries her hands in my hair

again, tugging slightly and sending shivers down my spine. I run my fingers down her neck and over her collarbone. Then I follow my lips down the exact same path, all the way down to her breasts.

She leans her body against the couch, arching her back. When I kiss her, she digs her fingers into my back. Our mouths become one as our tongues intertwine.

Suddenly, she pushes me away.

"What's wrong?" I ask as she sits up and throws her head between her legs.

Her body makes a loud heaving sound and she throws up.

"Are you okay?" I ask, pulling her hair out of her face.

"I'm sorry," she mumbles and throws up again.

"It's okay," I repeat myself over and over again. "It's fine. I just want you to feel better."

I run over to the kitchen and pour her a glass of water. After helping her to the bedroom, I tuck her into bed. I pull the trashcan over just in case.

"Thank you so much," she mumbles as I turn off the lights.

After cleaning up the couch and the floor, I throw away the paper towels and leave her apartment.

27

AURORA

The following morning I wake up early and decide to surprise Franklin with some coffee and bagels. I did not spend the night with him, but instead went back to my apartment as soon as Chelsea and Henry left. But Henry texted me and told me about the money that he gave Henry. I know that it's not much to Franklin, but I am still shocked by his generosity. It means so much to Henry.

I am so taken aback by his kindness I start to wonder if I'm wrong about him. Perhaps, he's not as terrible a person as I had made him out to be.

The truth is that I don't actually know very

much about Franklin. I thought all of this time that we have spent together would enlighten me about who he really is, but it hasn't. And every little bit just adds to the mystery.

The doorman waves me through and the elevator attendant makes small talk about the weather as we ride up.

I walk in and put the breakfast on the kitchen table. Instead of leaving it in the brown paper bag, I lay everything out on serving dishes, the bagels, the different types of cream cheese, and the fruit.

I don't actually know what kind of bagels or fruit or even breakfast Franklin likes, but I figure today is as good a day as any to find out.

After everything is set up, I walk down the hallway to his bedroom and quietly open the door. That's when I see *them*.

Franklin is spread-eagled on the bed completely nude and a svelte brunette is laying under the sheet, right next to him, facing away from me.

For a moment, I'm tempted to not make a scene. I consider simply sneaking out of the room, tiptoeing back out of the door and not ever talking about this again.

But then, I spot the hundred-thousand dollar watch that's on the dresser. Before I realize what I'm doing, I grab it and slam it to the floor.

They jump up, startled.

"What, what are you doing there?" Franklin roars. "What are you doing with my watch?"

"Who is that?" I demand to know.

The girl waves shyly to me and then quickly starts to get dressed and gather her things. She finds her dress on the banister and her underwear on the couch all the way across the room.

"Aren't you going to introduce me?" I ask. Franklin doesn't respond.

"Hi, I'm Aurora Tate. His fiancée. And you are?" I extend my hand demonstratively to her.

"You're Aurora Tate?" she gasps, stopping the search for her bra.

I spot something black and lacy on top of the dresser and hand it to her.

Shit, I should not have told her my name, I realize when it's too late.

"I'm Lindsey," she says, giving me a limp shake of the hand. "I'm leaving now."

"No, that's okay, stay. I brought you guys some breakfast," I say.

"Is that why you're here?" Franklin asks.

With anyone else, he would have the decency to put on his pants, but not him. He just stands there, completely nude, challenging me with his gaze.

"Yeah. Henry told me what a nice thing you did and I just wanted to come here and thank you for being such a wonderful guy," I say sarcastically.

When I walk away from him, he catches me by the front door. I open the door and he slams it shut. When I reach for it again, he again stops me.

"I'm sorry, okay? Is that what you want to hear?"

"I don't want to hear anything."

"Are you serious? I had to practically force you to even kiss me! What do you expect me to do?"

"You are such an asshole!"

"I don't know where we stand," he says. "You don't even seem to want to marry me."

"I don't! You've got that right."

He takes a step away from me.

"Do you want to call this off?" he asks after a moment.

I shrug.

Yes, of course the answer is yes. If he were anyone else then he would already know that.

"In that case," he says, "the deal is off."

"What deal?"

"Tate Media. I don't want it. I'm not gonna go through with the offer."

"No, you have to," I plead, hating the way that my voice cracks in the middle.

"I don't have to do anything. You don't want to marry me because you think I'm a cheating asshole? Well, two can play that game. I don't wanna marry you because I think your company is worthless and you are still in love with your ex-boyfriend. How about that? What do you think about that?"

"You can't pull your offer," I say, shaking my head.

"Why not?"

"That will make the stock price drop to nothing. We will lose everything."

"You'll have money to spare," he scoffs.

"All of our investors lose everything, and all of the people who have their pensions tied up in the company and in the shares will lose everything."

"What do I care about them?" he asks, shaking his head.

"No, you do care. I know you do," I insist.

When he walks back to his bedroom, I follow him.

I wait for him to get dressed before saying anything else.

"Why did you do that?" I ask. "Who is she?"

"Just some girl I met in the club a while ago. When you didn't stay last night, I called her up and she was down to party."

I turn away from him and wrap my arms around myself.

"What's the big deal? It's not like this is a real marriage?"

"I thought you wanted it to be."

"Well, clearly you don't."

"Franklin, I don't really understand what we're doing here. Why do you want to get married? Why do you want to marry me?"

I follow him out to the kitchen and he leans against the island. Popping a grape into his mouth, he chews it up before looking at me again.

"I don't know why," he says, taking another grape, this time chewing with his mouth open. "Maybe it's because you were the only one whoever said no."

There isn't anywhere to go from here. After I leave his apartment, I walk straight home but when I get there, I can't bring myself to go upstairs.

So, I just keep walking in circles.

When I get hungry, I pop into a local vegan restaurant and have some lunch. My head is in a fog.

Why did I go there? I wonder. What did I even expect from him?

I guess a part of me thought that maybe we could actually make this marriage work.

Maybe it didn't start out under the best of circumstances, but that doesn't mean that we couldn't be happy.

But seeing her there, I realize that if he wasn't happy with me then he would just turn to someone else.

We don't have anything in common.

He sees me only as something to possess.

Would that ever change? I have no idea.

How is your mom doing? I text Henry.

Okay, I guess, considering the circumstances. He texts back.

When I pick up my phone and call him, he answers on the first ring.

"Can I see you?" I ask. "I have something to tell you."

28

HENRY

I don't know why I'm going back there. I only got home around four in the morning, but when Aurora calls and asks to see me, I lie and say that I'm in the city already.

I want to see her.

I want to touch her.

At the very least, I want to be in the same room with her. Video chat isn't enough.

There's a screen separating us and I need to make that distance go away.

I take a deep breath when I walk up to her apartment. I don't know what to expect.

She may not want to talk to me about

anything personal or anything to do with us at all.

She may want to talk about my mother or worse yet Franklin. I have to be ready for that.

But no matter how much I try I can't seem to make the jitters go away.

Aurora shows me inside and offers me some food from the hors d'oeuvres that she has set out on the kitchen island.

There are chips, crisps, fruits, and vegetables.

I'm really hungry and I make myself a small plate.

She offers me something to drink, and we split a cider.

She asks about my mother and I tell her that nothing has changed since last night. I bring up the money that Franklin has given me and thank her as well.

"That was all him," she reassures me.

Then she stops talking and looks down at her hands.

"What's going on? Are you okay?"

"I have to tell you something. I wasn't

going to but now something has happened and I am more lost than before."

"Yes, of course, you can tell me anything," I say.

She shakes her head and buries her face in her palms.

"What's going on?" I ask, wrapping my arm around her shoulder. "Did something happen? Did he do something to you?"

She lifts her head and looks into my eyes.

"Our marriage is a sham," she says quietly.

I exhale slowly.

"Did you catch him cheating on you?" I ask.

I know Franklin well enough to know his reputation and to know how he treats women. I thought that his feelings for her were stronger than his basic urges, but now I realize that nothing has changed. Once an asshole, always an asshole.

"Yes, he did," she says, "but it's not about that."

"What are you talking about?"

"This whole thing has been a lie right from the beginning," she says. Her voice cracks in the middle of each word, as she inhales her sobs.

I wait patiently for her to continue.

But she doesn't say anything else. I wait some more, eventually kneeling down next to her and just holding her while she cries.

"My father was arrested for insider trading and a few other charges. He isn't well and as soon as he was in custody, he had a heart attack," Aurora says after moment. "That's when my mom told me about the arrangement."

"What arrangement?"

"They have been trying to sell Tate Media for a while to pay off its debts, but they didn't have any takers. My father has been stealing money from the pension funds and if the company goes under then there won't be any way to pay any of those people back. They would lose all of the retirements, and they're not wealthy. They're people like your mom who have worked their whole lives and want to retire and live out their golden years in some peace and stability."

I nod my head, listening carefully.

"The only way I could help them and

help my father is if I agreed to do something that I never thought I would."

I shake my head, not wanting to believe the words that are coming out of her mouth.

"I had to say yes. That was the only way he was going to buy the company and save everyone's jobs. It was the only way that I could help my father and preserve my family's legacy."

"Say yes to what?" I ask.

"He wanted to marry me. Apparently, I am the only woman who has ever said no to him and that's the only reason he wanted to make me his wife."

"I don't understand," I say, shaking my head.

"Our whole engagement is a farce," she says. "We were never dating. He just wanted to be engaged and he wanted me to marry him and in exchange he would save Tate Media."

"What happened to your father's case?" I ask.

'I don't know exactly. The lawyers aren't telling me much. But everyone just seems happy that the charges were dropped because Franklin pulled a few strings."

"Why are you telling me this *now*?" I ask. "Did something happen?"

She gets up and paces around the room, nervously cracking her knuckles.

"I thought that I could make it work," she says after a moment. "I thought that maybe this could be a real marriage. But then this morning, I walked in on him with another woman. After I left last night –"

"You didn't stay there last night?" I ask. A pang of guilt overcomes me as I think back to my own evening with Chelsea.

"No, nothing has ever happened between us yet. Nothing significant, anyway."

I find that hard to believe, but I don't say anything.

"Why not?" I ask.

"It just never felt right. Every time that we've been together it just felt like I had to be there. I never wanted to be with him. You have to believe me."

She looks up at me with big wide eyes.

"Of course, I believe you," I say, draping

my arm around her shoulders and pulling her close to me.

I inhale the sweet aroma of her hair and bury my face in it. She holds onto me tightly before letting herself go. Her sobs are quiet at first but they grow bigger and louder.

"I don't know why I am crying," she says, pulling away from me occasionally but continuing to cry. "It's so stupid, I feel so dumb."

"No, please don't. I'm here for you. No matter what."

I hold her for a long time that evening. I hold her as she tells me that she never lost any bet that day, but he forced her to make dinner for all of us. I hold her as she tells me how stupid she felt seeing a woman in bed with him.

"Will you stay with me tonight?" Aurora asks, brushing the tears off her cheeks and pulling her hair into a bun. "I just need someone to be here. I just really don't wanna be alone."

"Yes," I whisper, "of course."

29

AURORA

I ask him to stay here because he's the person that I always think of when I need someone to be there for me. He's the only one that ever mattered and he's the only one that will ever matter.

I don't know what I'm gonna do about Franklin or my impending wedding. I don't know how I can save my father, the company, everyone's pension, and my own sanity at the same time.

All I know is that I want to spend the night with Henry.

He agrees to stay, but we decide that it's best if he sleeps in the guest room. When I get the blankets out of the linen closet, he follows behind me and helps me reach the ones at the top.

"Here you go," he says, handing me a bundle of gray tweed.

He stands a little too close and suddenly the casual moment morphs into something a lot more significant.

He looks into my eyes and I look into his.

I reach up and run my fingers along his jawline and he reaches over and brushes a hair off my neck.

"I love you," he whispers.

His voice is soft and effervescent.

When I take a step closer to him, our bodies collide.

His mouth finds mine and my tongue searches for his. He runs his fingers down my neck. I press my body against him and push him into the wall.

Henry runs his tongue down my neck and over my collarbone. His hands cup my breasts. One of them makes its way up my shirt.

I toss my hair back and lose myself in the moment. He pulls off my shirt and I unbutton his.

I run my fingers down his perfect six pack and can't help but lick my lips. He puts his finger under my chin and tilts my head up, kissing me again.

Suddenly, I don't know where my body ends and where his begins. The rest of our clothes fall to the floor effortlessly.

A few moments later we are naked, standing in front of each other. I pull away, but only for a second to get a good look at him.

The light is low and alluring. I look down at my body, a little bit embarrassed, but when I look back up at him, I see nothing but desire in his eyes.

He runs his fingers over my breasts and down my stomach. I wonder if he has been alone with Chelsea yet and how my body compares to hers but push those thoughts away.

He's here with you now, I say to myself. That's all that matters.

Besides, right here, in this moment, I can see the way that he feels about me. He loves my body even though I don't. He wants me in the way that every woman wants to be wanted. He wants me just as much as I want him.

Henry takes my hand and leads me to my bedroom. He turns around on occasion, kissing the back of my hand and listening to my giggles.

When we cross the threshold into my bedroom, he takes me into his arms. He lifts me up, wraps my legs around his torso, and carries me to bed. I know that I've gained a few pounds yet he carries me as if I weigh as light as a feather.

His shoulders are wide and powerful. He has always liked to take care of his body and all the time spent in motel rooms has not had a detrimental effect on him.

The muscles going down his stomach are taut and spindly. I can see every single indentation of his six pack, including that impossibly perfect V going down toward his groin as if it were an arrow telling me where to focus my attention.

I grab onto his hard and perfectly round ass and pinch it when he drops me down to my feet.

"Seems like all of this time writing and

recording didn't stop you from spending time at the gym," I comment.

He laughs and a loose strand of hair falls into his face. I reach up and tuck it behind his ear.

"You know how I am," he says. "Whenever I get antsy or depressed, I like to punish myself at the gym. It's the only thing that makes me feel better."

"Are you telling me that this is a byproduct of our breakup?" I ask, smiling at the corner of my lips and pointing at his sick abs.

"Listen, you really broke my heart, what can I say?" He shrugs and pulls me on top of him.

Lying next to him, it feels like our bodies belong together. They know each other in every way that two people can possibly know each other and it's both familiar and sexy and impossible to resist.

"I'm sorry that I can't say the same." I laugh in a self-deprecating way, pointing to my love handles.

"Oh, no, I love your body just the way it is. Don't ever change."

I can't help but blush and look away from him. When he sees me shying away, he brings my chin up to his and presses his lips onto mine.

"I mean it," he says with utter seriousness. "If you want to change your body, you should, of course do it, but only if you wanna to do it for *yourself*. I find you incredibly attractive just the way you are. And don't you ever think otherwise."

I close my eyes and tilt my head back.

He starts to kiss me, running his tongue from my neck down my body.

I close my eyes and lose myself in the moment. He knows his way around my body and my legs open up for him.

Suddenly, every muscle relaxes and I let out a deep sigh of relief. This is who I belong with. This is who understands me and this is who loves me.

When he climbs on top of me, and drapes his strong body over me, I feel like I'm finally home. After a few moments, his kisses become more frantic and his thrusts become stronger.

We start to move as one. I put my head

back and arch my back. He goes deeper and deeper inside of me and then one moment I just let myself go completely.

I yell his name at the top of my lungs as he moans mine into my ear.

30

AURORA

The following morning, Henry and I make plans. Actually, we stay up all night making them.

"Whatever happens," he says, lying in bed next to me with his fingers running up my thighs, "you cannot marry him next week."

"I don't want to, of course not, but I need to speak to my father. I need to really try to figure out another plan."

"What's gonna happen with Tate Media if you pull out?"

"That's the thing, I don't really know. My parents pretty much kept me in the dark about stuff and that hasn't been the best thing as of recently."

"Even now?" he asks.

I give him a slight nod, averting my eyes.

"I don't understand. Why?" he asks.

"Well, to be honest, I've been kind of avoiding the whole situation. We've talked about it briefly, but a little bit too briefly and I've been too embarrassed to bring it up."

"I'm really sorry," he says, squeezing my hand.

I shake my head and pull away from him. I pull at the bedsheet, adjusting it more securely around my naked breasts.

"I guess I just didn't want to think about it. I wanted to get to know him better and maybe try to work it out. That's one of the reasons why I didn't tell you what was going on," I admit. "I really wanted to make it work. I thought that maybe we could actually fall in love and maybe I could mold this awful situation into an actual relationship."

"And now?" he asks.

"Now, I just realize that I shouldn't have ever even tried. We are two different people and we have nothing in common. Besides, he's… When I walked in on him with that woman, I just knew that he would never really care about me in that way."

"Like the way I care about you?" he asks. I nod.

"I love you, Aurora. I've loved you ever since I first laid my eyes on you. You're the only person that I have ever felt that way about and when we broke up, I actually felt my heart break into pieces."

I see a tear form in the corner of his eye.

Henry's not a particularly emotional person, but I have never seen him be this vulnerable before. If he had ever opened up to me like this before, we would've never broken up.

"I should not have let my work get in between our relationship. There's nothing more important than us," he says.

"No, I was the one who was selfish. I should not have just stewed in my anger and gotten so angry with you."

"I forgot about your graduation," he says.

I think about that one for a moment.

"Okay," I say. "You win. You're the bigger asshole."

He grabs my hand and pulls me toward him. He kisses me on the lips, burying his fingers in my hair.

"Do you forgive me?" he asks, not pulling his lips too far away from mine.

"No," I say, smiling.

He kisses me harder. His tongue intertwines with mine as he leans me back on the bed. Running his fingers over my nipples, he leans down and puts one in between his teeth.

"Do you forgive me now?" he asks.

"Well, now I feel like I'm answering under duress," I joke.

He doesn't let go and wraps his mouth around my breast.

"How about now?" he asks.

I tilt my head back and give out a little moan. He slides his hand in between my thighs and buries his fingers deep within me.

"How about now?" he asks.

"Yes," I whisper.

"Yes, what?" He pushes me, swirling his fingers around and around.

"I forgive you," I moan.

It doesn't take me long to get there. He spreads my legs open and I welcome him inside.

We move together in short little thrusts until that familiar warm sensation starts to course through my body. It's hard to imagine that there was a time when I couldn't orgasm with him. Or a time when I wasn't completely comfortable with him touching every single part of me, no matter how private and personal.

Drenched in sweat, we lie in each other's arms for a long time after that. I cradle his head and play with his hair as he makes little figure eights around my belly button.

This time, we don't talk about the future.

This time, we just lose ourselves in the moment.

I don't get dressed until later that evening. I don't even get out of bed until half an hour before I'm supposed to meet him.

"I know that you are really dreading this," Henry says, "but you really have to talk to him. I'm sure that your father doesn't want you to do anything you don't want to do. He loves you and he's the one person who will help you figure this out."

31

AURORA

On my way over to my father's apartment on Fifth Avenue, I force myself to put a positive spin on the situation. There must be another way out of this.

No one has arranged marriages anymore, at least not among the wealthy elite of New York City. My father loves me and he wouldn't want me to marry anyone who wasn't a great match.

I tell myself this and about ten other mantras, hoping against hope that I'm right.

The guest services assistant downstairs calls him and tells him that I'm here. A few moments later, the elevator arrives.

My father likes to stay in this apartment whenever he gets 'too tired of being married,' as he calls it. I don't know the nature of my parents' relationship, as far as all of the nitty-gritty details go, but to say that it's a somewhat complicated situation would be an understatement.

My parents have a 10,000 square-foot apartment that they share in the city along with an estate in the Hamptons and a few other houses around the country, but they also have their own personal apartments in the city whenever they want to get away.

My father refers to his apartment as a man cave, somewhat ironically, and ever since he started doing that, my mom started referring to her 5,000 square-foot apartment as her she shed, completely ironically.

My father's apartment is around 7000 square feet and contains three floors as well as two elevators that go in between them. He had to get special permission from the city to build, or rather to renovate and combine five apartments into one. After he found the right connections, he managed to get it done.

I think that what my father likes best about his place is that it is decorated specifically to his taste. Everything is black-and-white with traces of gold, basically exactly what you would think of as a bachelor pad. There's even a large pool table near the entrance and all of the toilets are gold plated.

"Hey there, honey," Dad says, throwing his arm around me and giving me a warm hug. I haven't seen him much since he got out of the hospital, but he looks good.

His tan from earlier in the year has faded a bit and I can tell that he hasn't been going to the gym or getting spray tanned like he usually does in the winter.

"You look good," I say. "How are you feeling?"

"Actually a lot better. That was quite a scare, wasn't it?"

"Yes, it was. We actually thought we were going to lose you."

"Who, me? Come on now, it would take a lot more than a little heart attack in jail to take me out."

"I hope so," I say, giving him a smile.

"So, would you like to get something to eat?" I ask.

I look around the spotless marble kitchen with two enormous islands. I don't see a single edible thing anywhere in sight.

"Actually, Rafael made us something to eat before he left for the day."

"Oh, okay," I say, rather surprised.

My father goes to the refrigerator and pulls out a tray of pre-made food.

"I'll just pop this onto the skillet and it'll be ready in ten minutes."

My mouth nearly drops open.

"Hey, don't look so surprised," my father says, tossing his salt and pepper hair and shrugging in that casual unassuming way that only he does.

"Hey, I'm sorry, I just don't think I've ever seen you cook like ever…"

"Well, I'm a new man, or at least trying to become one."

After throwing the food into the pan and moving it around with the spatula, he asks, "What's going on with you?"

I don't really know how to answer him, not right away. I want to enjoy this moment, without complicating it with what is at stake.

But then I realize that I can't *not* talk about it. That has been the core of the issue.

"I'm glad you're feeling better," I say. "I was really worried before."

"I know you were, honey. And I really didn't want you to be."

"It's just that it happened so quickly. Everything seemed to just take a turn for the worse. I really wish that you and Mom had told me what was really going on... Before."

"We didn't want to involve you. We didn't want you to worry. We wanted you to keep thinking that everything was fine."

"But you couldn't work it all out. And then it got really out of hand, didn't it?"

"What do you mean?" Dad asks.

"Well, they came and arrested you and you didn't even know about it."

"Yes, that was a surprise. But then they dropped the charges," he says. "Thanks to Franklin. See, things always work out."

"No, Daddy, they don't. At least not without consequences to other people."

"What are you talking about?"

"Well, I don't think this will come as a surprise to you but I don't really want to marry him. Actually I don't want to marry him *at all*."

The plastic smile vanishes and a more severe and serious expression emerges.

"Honey, don't say that," Dad says. "That's a very dangerous thing to say."

"What are you talking about?"

"If you don't marry him, then we will lose everything. Everything that your mother and I have built up over all of these years."

I shake my head. I don't know what to say.

Of course, I don't want him to lose everything, but I also don't want to marry someone that I don't want to be in the same room with and do so without an exit strategy.

"You know about the people who have their pensions tied up with Tate Media, right?"

I nod.

"They're not like us," he says. "They don't have houses to sell and stock options to liquidate and all of those other things that protect us from the so-called real world.

"They just have their measly one hundred, two hundred grand tied up in a company that's going to go up in flames unless you do something to save it."

"But why is it up to me? You never wanted me to be involved before and suddenly it's all up to me?"

"Honey, I fucked up. I'll be the first one to admit that. I took money that I shouldn't have out of the company's coffers. I spent all of it. I thought I'd be able to put it back, but I couldn't. That's what all of those people were investigating. They know exactly what I did and the only way to deal with the situation now is to have Franklin's people cover it up and to have Tate Media be absorbed into OMS, his parents' company."

I shake my head. I get off of the barstool and pace around the room.

"Okay, let's say I marry him. What then? What's my end goal? How do I get divorced and get the company back on its feet? How do we make any of that happen?"

My father shakes his head.

"The simple answer is that you don't," he says quietly.

My eyes open wide and I stare at him, finding it hard to believe that he's saying this.

"Do you want me to actually stay married?"

"I want you to marry him and I want you to try to make a good life with him. After some time, he will grow the company and bring it back up to his feet. Those people will not lose their jobs and they will not lose their pensions. And who knows, maybe the two of you can be happy?"

"And if we're not?"

"If you're not, then you wouldn't be the first couple to find happiness... Elsewhere."

Tears well up in my eyes and I turn away from him to not let him see me cry.

"Honey, I'm sorry, I didn't want to make you upset," my father says.

"I'm sorry, I shouldn't let this get to me," I say, taking a deep breath and trying to push away my tears.

"What's wrong? Tell me what you're thinking."

I flip my head back.

"I'm not going to marry him," I say.

"You have to," Dad says calmly. His voice is so monotone and detached that it sends shivers down my spine.

"No, I can't. This isn't going to solve your problem and it's just going to add to mine. I want more for my life than to be married to some man who I don't even like."

My father plates our dinner. We sit down silently at the dining room table, him at the head and me at the chair next to him. Without another word, I start to eat. I'm hungry and thirsty and disappointed and I hope that this will alleviate at least some of that.

"I know that this is a difficult thing for you to do," Dad says after finishing all the broccoli. "I know this is a difficult thing for you to do since your mother and I have never really asked you to do anything for us."

"It's not about that," I say, glancing up at him." I just don't think that you can ask someone to marry someone they don't love as what exactly? A favor?"

"I have to tell you something," he says with a heavy sigh.

"What?"

"I promised your mother that I wouldn't and I don't like to break my promises to her but in this case, I think I have to."

"What?"

He takes a deep breath and finishes his glass of wine.

"I'm not just facing a long prison sentence. It's more than that."

"What are you talking about?"

"They're going to kill me," he says quietly.

I lean over to hear him better, unsure as to whether his words came out properly.

"What did you say?"

"My life is in danger," he says after a long pause. "If this doesn't happen, if you don't go through with this wedding, they're going to kill me."

"Who?"

"I owe a lot of people a lot of debts. They are the kind of debts that you can't default on, they're the kind of debts that you can bankrupt yourself over. And they're the kind of debts that you have to pay back unless you want someone to chop you up in little pieces and send you home in a box to your wife and children."

I lean closer and put my hand on his forearm. What is he talking about I wonder to myself? Who is this person who I used to think that I knew?

For a second, I wonder if he's actually telling me the truth but when I look into his eyes and into that lost and concerned and frightened expression on his face, I know that he is.

"Franklin Parks is a very bad man," my father says. "I know that, probably a lot more than you do. I would not be asking you to do this for me if I knew that there was even a chance that there was another way out of this."

"Why didn't you tell me this before?"

He shrugs and looks away but continues to hold my hand.

"I thought that maybe there was a chance that you could fall in love. I thought that maybe there was a chance that he could be a good man for you and you two could actually be happy. I didn't want to send you into this arrangement with your guard up. Maybe that was a mistake."

"Daddy," I say. I don't call him this often, and I haven't called him this in a long time.

"I love Henry," I whisper.

New tears start to roll down my cheeks.

"I caught Franklin with another woman yesterday morning and I went to talk to Henry and we started to reminisce and…" My voice trails off.

"I love him and we should have never broken up. I want to get back together with him."

"I know that you love him, honey. I didn't think that you ever stopped. And maybe you could be together sometime after this. I thought that maybe Franklin could be faithful to you, but now I doubt that. So, maybe in the future, you and Henry can try to give it a go again."

I shake my head, no, no, no.

"I know that what I'm asking you to do is an impossible thing. I know that it is unfair and awful and old-fashioned and completely out of line. But please know that I would never ask you to do this if I thought for a second there was some other way out of it. My life is in danger and they're going to kill me if this doesn't happen."

"Who? Who is going to kill you?" I ask. "Franklin wants to buy the company and he may want me, but I don't think that he will kill you if I refuse."

"It's not just Franklin. He's my ally. But he's only my ally if you become his wife. After that, especially if you break his heart, he'll have no reason to stay on my side."

Dad keeps going in circles and still avoiding the crux of the issue. I press him, but he refuses to tell me anymore.

"I can't," he says, shaking his head with tears of his own now welling up in his eyes. "If I tell you anymore, then your life will be in danger as well. I can't protect you much, but this is the least that I can do and I will at least do this."

I WALK BACK to my apartment with a heavy heart. I thought that he would be on my side and he would try to help me figure this out, but now I realize that he is in well over his head.

I don't know what I'm going to do. I'm certain that my father is not lying, but I still don't know the details of what I'm facing.

I don't know why his life is in danger and I don't know why Franklin is the only one who can help him.

When I get to the bottom of my building, I keep going. I want to see Henry more than anything and yet I don't have the heart to tell him what happened.

What would happen if I were to marry Franklin? I wonder. What would my life be like?

While before I thought that marrying him would force me to come up with an exit strategy, now I wonder if I'll have to stay married to him forever in order to make my life work out.

32

HENRY

I still think back to that moment when I watched her leave the apartment to go see her father. I thought that talking to him would help fix this, but it just makes things worse.

I didn't see Aurora after that. Whatever her father said to her solidified her decision to marry Franklin and to separate herself from me.

I don't speak to her again.

I wait and wait and wait and then the doorman comes up and knocks on the door and tells me that Aurora has asked me to leave the apartment. She did not even have the decency to tell me this to my face. I call and I text and I email and she does not reply.

Eventually, I receive a note that says that she will always love me but she has to do what she has to do to protect her family.

As I watch her walk down the aisle on television, toward his beaming and arrogant face, I wonder what I could've done to stop this from happening.

I'm angry.

Pissed off. But it's more than that.

I know that whatever the Tate family has going on, it is dangerous and beyond Aurora's control.

She thinks that she can be safe by climbing into the eye of the hurricane, but she doesn't realize that to ever get out she'll have to go through it again.

One thing is for sure, I will love her for as long as I have breath in my body. It doesn't matter that she may not feel the same way.

I will do everything that I can to protect her, even if it means keeping her safe from afar.

But to do this, I have to find out the

truth. I need to know exactly what Franklin Parks has over her father. I need to know why she is walking down that aisle. And I will find out the truth if it's the last thing that I do.

THANK you for reading Lethal Wedding. I hope you are enjoying Henry and Aurora's story. Their love story concludes in the third and final book of this epic trilogy.

One-click FATAL MARRIAGE Now!

I was forced into this marriage to save my father's life and our family's empire, but my husband has other plans.

He wants to sell Tate Media for parts and make himself billions in the process.

. . .

THE ONLY WAY I can stop him is to expose his not-so-secret life.

FRANKLIN PARKS IS A **MONSTER.** We have all heard the rumors, but anyone who has dared to stand up to him has been silenced. Now, it's my turn.

HE IS PROTECTED by all of the rich and powerful because he protects their secrets in return.

THERE'S only person I can trust: Henry Asher, the love of my life.

I SHOULDN'T GET him involved. It's too dangerous, but we can't stay away from each other.

CAN I escape my marriage and save my

legacy or will I lose everything and everyone I love in the process?

One-click FATAL MARRIAGE Now!

SIGN up for my **newsletter** to find out when I have new books!

You can also join my Facebook group, **Charlotte Byrd's Reader Club**, for exclusive giveaways and sneak peaks of future books.

I appreciate you sharing my books and telling your friends about them. Reviews help readers find my books! Please leave a review on your favorite site.

CONNECT WITH CHARLOTTE BYRD

Sign up for my **newsletter** to find out when I have new books!

You can also join my Facebook group, **Charlotte Byrd's Reader Club**, for exclusive giveaways and sneak peaks of future books.

I appreciate you sharing my books and telling your friends about them. Reviews help readers find my books! Please leave a review on your favorite site.

Sign up for my newsletter: https://www.subscribepage.com/byrdVIPList

Join my Facebook Group: https://www.facebook.com/groups/276340079439433/

Bonus Points: Follow me on BookBub and Goodreads!

ALSO BY CHARLOTTE BYRD

All books are available at ALL major retailers! If you can't find it, please email me at charlotte@charlotte-byrd.com

Wedlocked Trilogy
Dangerous Engagement
Lethal Wedding
Fatal Wedding

Tell me Series
Tell Me to Stop
Tell Me to Go
Tell Me to Stay

Tell Me to Run
Tell Me to Fight
Tell Me to Lie

Tangled Series
Tangled up in Ice
Tangled up in Pain
Tangled up in Lace
Tangled up in Hate
Tangled up in Love

Black Series
Black Edge
Black Rules
Black Bounds
Black Contract
Black Limit

Lavish Trilogy
Lavish Lies
Lavish Betrayal
Lavish Obsession

Standalone Novels
Debt

Offer

Unknown

Dressing Mr. Dalton

ABOUT CHARLOTTE BYRD

Charlotte Byrd is the bestselling author of romantic suspense novels. She has sold over 600,000 books and has been translated into five languages.

She lives near Palm Springs, California with her husband, son, and a toy Australian Shepherd who hates water. She is addicted to books and streaming shows and she loves hot weather and crystal blue water.

Write her here:

charlotte@charlotte-byrd.com

Check out her books here:

www.charlotte-byrd.com

Connect with her here:

www.facebook.com/charlottebyrdbooks

www.instagram.com/charlottebyrdbooks

www.twitter.com/byrdauthor

Want to hear about new releases, free books and get exclusive giveaways?

Sign up for my newsletter!

Sign up for my newsletter: https://www.
subscribepage.com/byrdVIPList

Join my Facebook Group: https://www.
facebook.com/groups/276340079439433/

Bonus Points: Follow me on BookBub and
Goodreads!

 facebook.com/charlottebyrdbooks

 twitter.com/byrdauthor

 instagram.com/charlottebyrdbooks

 bookbub.com/profile/charlotte-byrd

Printed in Great Britain
by Amazon